THE SUN
WILL
COME OUT

THE SUN WILL COME OUT

JOANNE LEVY

ORCA BOOK PUBLISHERS

Published in Canada and the United States in 2021 by Orca Book Publishers.
orcabook.com

Library and Archives Canada Cataloguing in Publication
Title: The sun will come out / Joanne Levy.
Names: Levy, Joanne, author.
Identifiers: Canadiana (print) 20200335359 | Canadiana (ebook) 2020033543X | ISBN 9781459825871 (softcover) | ISBN 9781459812475 (PDF) | ISBN 9781459812482 (EPUB)
Classification: LCC PS8623.E9592 S86 2021 | DDC jc813/.6—dc23

Library of Congress Control Number: 2020944961

Summary: In this novel for middle-grade readers, painfully shy Beatrice Gelman ends up at summer camp all by herself.

Orca Book Publishers is committed to reducing the consumption of nonrenewable resources in the making of our books. We make every effort to use materials that support a sustainable future.

Orca Book Publishers gratefully acknowledges the support for its publishing programs provided by the following agencies: the Government of Canada, the Canada Council for the Arts and the Province of British Columbia through the BC Arts Council and the Book Publishing Tax Credit.

Cover artwork by Brayden Sato
Cover design by Rachel Page
Edited by Tanya Trafford

Printed and bound in Canada.

24 23 22 21 • 1 2 3 4

For the wonderful people at PJ Library
and PJ Our Way, without whom this book
would still be packed away under my bed.

ONE

Frankie Ferstein and I have ALWAYS been best friends. I would say since we were born, because our mothers are friends and even had us around the same time. I can't say for sure that we were BFFs back in our mothers' wombs but we probably were.

Since we were old enough to hang out, Frankie and I have been inseparable. We've had our birthday parties together, done our homework together, shopped for clothes together—*everything*.

So, of course, it made sense that we were going to summer camp together. I mean, we had always gone to *day* camp together, but this year would be different. We were going to Camp Shalom, which was a *sleepover* camp. Four weeks of unsupervised fun. Well, unsupervised by our own parents. It wasn't like they were going to throw us all together to run around on our own like wild animals or anything.

But still, four weeks of sleeping in cabins, arts and crafts, and outdoor sports? Yes, please.

One Friday after school, a couple of weeks before school was done for the year, Frankie and I were lying on her bed doing homework. We had about an hour before her mom got home and Frankie had to help with Shabbat dinner.

By *lying on her bed doing homework*, I mean lying on her bed, her scrolling through her iPad, and me looking at YouTube videos of horses on my phone. This late in the year, teachers knew giving us serious homework was just bad form.

"So…Bea?" Frankie asked.

"Yeah?" I didn't look up from the screen.

"We need to talk. I…uh…I wasn't supposed to tell you this, but we're best friends, so I have to."

Her tone got my attention. "Tell me what?"

"It's about this summer."

I instantly perked up. "Yeah, it's going to be awesome! I hope we get to go on canoe trips like your brother did."

She cocked her head. "You sure spend a lot of time talking to Jeremy. You're not going to be chasing him all around at camp, are you?"

I felt my face heat up but gave her an exasperated look. "No! It's *research*, Frankie. So we know what to expect when *we* go to camp. Please."

She frowned for a second, then shook her head and took a big, deep breath. "So. About that."

My stomach did a complete flop. Something bad was coming. Even my internal organs knew it. I just stared at Frankie, waiting for her to spill.

She looked down at her iPad and whispered something.

"What?" I asked—loudly, so she would take the hint to speak up.

"I'm not going. I'm going to Circle M camp instead."

I was stunned into complete and absolute silence.

"We always talked about going to Circle M," she said quickly. "You know how much I love horses."

We both *love horses*, I wanted to say, but couldn't. My throat had closed up, and my eyes began to fill with tears.

"How could you?" I tried to say, but my voice was gone. All that came out was a squeak.

Either Frankie read my lips or knew what I was saying because we were best friends, and best friends know what their best friends are trying to say even when they are only able to squeak.

"We *wanted* to go to Circle M," she said.

"Together," I said as I swiped away tears with the back of my hand. Because best friends do everything together or not at all. I couldn't even imagine camp without her. I couldn't even imagine a week without her, let alone a month without her. A month alone at a camp where I didn't know anyone.

She looked down at her iPad again. "Well, it's not my fault that your parents can't afford it. I really want to go. You should be happy for me that I can."

I stared at her. I couldn't believe she'd just said that to me.

Before she could say any more horrible things, I ran out of her room and didn't stop running until I got to my house, four blocks away.

I managed to get inside the door before the waterworks really began. I went to drop my backpack on the bench beside the door like I always did, then realized I had left it at Frankie's house.

That made me cry harder.

Mom came out of the kitchen. She'd obviously

heard me, because, I'm not going to lie, I was crying pretty loudly. I probably sounded like a cat that had been kicked. Hard.

"Honey, what's wrong?"

I sniffed and wiped my arm across my eyes and started to tell her, but all that came out of my mouth was wailing and hiccups, and it probably sounded something like, "Sh…Sh…Frankieaaaaaaa. Cir… (hic)…cir…Circle…(hic)…emmmmm."

Mom knelt down and wrapped her arms around me. Somehow she had understood my blubbery warbling. Moms are good at that. "Oh honey, I'm so sorry. Your dad and I were going to tell you about that this weekend." She huffed out a breath. "Frankie's parents weren't supposed to tell her so soon. They'd had her on a waiting list, and a spot just opened up."

"But…but…" I said into Mom's hair between hiccups.

She squeezed me tighter. "I'm so sorry, Bea."

"But…ca…ca…can't…can't I go too? Pleeeeeease?"

Mom pulled away and sat back on her heels. She looked sad as she shook her head. "I'm sorry, Bea. We just can't afford it this year. It's more than double the cost of Camp Shalom."

There had to be a way. I would do *any*thing. "I'll drop out of Hebrew school," I offered.

Mom rolled her eyes. "Nice try."

Busted. Mom knew I hate Hebrew school, but there was no way I'd get out of that. It's not that I don't like being Jewish. I just hate sitting in MORE school after regular school and on Sundays. A girl can only handle so much school, no matter how interesting the topics might be.

She sighed. "I know you're disappointed, but there just isn't enough money, Bea. You know your dad and I went to Camp Shalom, and we both had great experiences there, meeting other kids from all over the world."

She put a big smile on her face, but her sales pitch had worked a lot better when Frankie was coming with me.

"What about if I don't go to any movies and donate my savings?"

"I'm sorry. It wouldn't be enough."

And that was it. I was going to be stuck alone at stupid Camp Shalom while Frankie got to ride horses all summer. It was so unfair!

"Maybe you should get a job then," I blurted out. "Maybe if you had a *real* job, I could go!"

I realized right away that I'd made a huge mistake, but it was too late to take it back.

Mom's eyes got very narrow as she stood up and crossed her arms. "I do have a real job, Bea. Not only am I your and Stevie's mom, which, believe me, is a full-time career, but I am also an artist. Not everything worth doing has to be something that earns money."

I didn't say a word, only scowled at her.

"Bea," she continued, "remember when we went to the art gallery? Remember how much you enjoyed seeing all that arwork? What would happen if all those artists had decided not to create because they weren't being paid enough?"

I shrugged. Maybe I'd appreciate my mother's art more if she painted horses and not just the blobs and smears that she called abstract.

"Anyway," Mom went on. "Camp Shalom is a great camp, and it isn't cheap either. Maybe you should feel lucky that you get to go; some kids are going to day camps or none at all."

She didn't get it. I didn't think she was even trying to understand.

"I don't care about other kids!" I yelled. "I don't understand why you have to paint all day when other kids' moms have jobs where they earn enough money to send their kids to horse camp." I was speaking of Frankie's mom, of course. She's a doctor, not a wannabe artist.

Mom didn't say anything more, but I could tell she was super mad. Her lips were pressed together in a tight line like she was trying to keep her words in.

But I wasn't done. And I wasn't keeping anything in.

"And how am I supposed to go to camp without Frankie? How am I supposed to go anywhere without my best friend?"

Mom opened her mouth. "Bea…"

But then I realized what was really bothering me.

Frankie didn't have any problem going to camp *without me*. My best friend had totally betrayed me.

I began to cry again. "This is going to be the worst summer EVER!"

Mom stepped toward me again, but I dodged her and ran to my bedroom. I needed to be alone to wallow in all my misery.

TWO

About an hour later there was a knock at my bedroom door. I ignored it.

Another, louder rap came seconds later.

It was my dad. "Bea?"

I didn't respond.

"Beatrice. I know you're in there."

I sat up on my bed against the headboard and sighed. When Dad called me Beatrice, and in that tone, it was in my best interest to obey. "Fine. Come in."

Dad opened the door. He was still wearing his work clothes. That was not a good sign. He always changed out of them as soon as he got home. Mom must have gotten to him right at the front door.

"Hey," he said as he walked over and pulled out my desk chair to sit on.

I didn't look at him. "Hi."

"Listen, Bea. Your mom is pretty upset."

She's upset? I wanted to say. *She's not the one whose best friend gets to go to horse camp.* Pointing that out was not going to help my case, so I stayed quiet.

"You know she's working hard getting ready for her gallery show. I'm really proud of her and you should be too. Did you know that she worked two jobs while I was going to college? Now it's her turn to follow her passion. To suggest she get a 'real job' so you can go to horse camp is pretty selfish, don't you think?"

I looked down at my hands. "I just don't understand why Frankie gets to go and I don't. It's not fair."

"You're going to have a great time at Camp Shalom."

I crossed my arms. I seriously doubted it.

"Bea?" My dad's voice was firm. I knew the lecture wasn't over. "Bea? Look at me."

I did.

"Listen. Life isn't fair all of the time. Your mother and I work very hard, but it just isn't possible to send you to horse camp this year. I know you're disappointed about that and about Frankie going without you. We had hoped you girls could be together for your first time at sleepaway camp, but her parents decided they wanted to send her to Circle M, and there's nothing we can do about that. You'll make new friends at Camp Shalom. I promise."

"How can you know that? How can you promise I'll make friends?" Just the thought of going by myself made my face feel hot and tingly.

Dad smiled. "Because you're my Queen Bea. You're a great kid. You just need to get out of your shell a bit more and meet some new people. Maybe this is a good thing for you. Maybe this is your silver lining."

I failed to see how anything good could come of being abandoned by my best friend. Dad was always looking for the good things that come out of bad things. "How could this possibly be a silver lining?"

"Well, with Frankie being so outgoing, you've never had to really go out and meet people. You've always let her do all the talking and stayed in her shadow."

And this is a problem, why? Frankie likes *to talk. She* likes *being the center of attention.*

"I don't *want* to meet new people," I said in a tiny voice.

Dad reached over and squeezed my hand. "Aw, come on, Bea. I know you're shy, but just think of how much fun you'll have. By the end of the summer, you'll look back and see how great a time you had, even without Frankie there. I'm sure of it."

I wasn't. I wasn't sure of it *at all.*

"Just last week you were saying how excited you were about going to camp. How much you were looking forward to pottery classes and learning to kayak and going on canoe trips. Remember?"

"But that was when I thought I was doing those things *with Frankie.*"

"Bea," Dad said in *that* voice. The voice that meant he wasn't going to put up with me much longer. "I promise you will have fun. You and Frankie have been friends for a long time, but that doesn't mean you can't be friends with other people, does it?"

I shrugged, knowing I was fighting a losing battle. He took the shrug as my white flag of surrender.

"Good. Now come on," he said, standing up. "I need a shower before dinner, but first I think you owe your mother an apology. You really hurt her feelings."

I got up also. "I didn't mean to."

"You still need to tell her you're sorry."

"I know, Dad."

"BEA!" yelled Stevie from out in the hall. "MOM SAYS IT'S YOUR TURN TO SET THE TABLE!"

My seven-year-old brother has two volume settings, sleeping and maximum.

"Stevie," Dad said. "Down a notch or two, huh, buddy?"

"SORRY, DAD!"

I rolled my eyes.

Dad laughed. "Maybe you can take him to Camp Shalom with you this summer."

For a second I was horrified, until I realized he was joking.

I exhaled in relief. "Very funny!"

THREE

The next morning I was sitting in the den, watching *Animal Planet* and eating a bowl of cereal, when there was a knock at the front door. Mom was in the bathroom having a shower and Dad was still in bed, so I put my bowl down, headed to the front hall and took a peek out the window beside the door.

Frankie was standing on the porch, holding my backpack and bouncing from one foot to the other and back again—something she did when she was nervous.

I unlocked and opened the door.

"Hey," I said.

"Hey." She didn't look at me. "I brought your bag." She shoved it toward me.

"Thanks," I said. Then, to fill the awkward silence, I added, "I guess I'll see you at school on Monday."

"Wait, Bea," she said as I began to shut the door.

Yeah, I was still mad. But I froze, waiting to hear what she had to say.

"I hope you aren't mad at me."

I opened my mouth, then closed it.

"Bea? Please, you know how much I wanted to go to Circle M." She was still looking at the ground.

"Yeah, I do. As much as *I* wanted to go to Circle M."

She looked up at me finally. "Why can't you be happy for me?"

I crossed my arms. "Oh, I don't know. Maybe because you betrayed me?"

Frankie's lower lip quivered. "Bea, I wish so hard you could go to Circle M. I *want* you to be there with me. Do you think I wished for *this*—to go by myself? This is *agony* for me, don't you understand?"

I didn't. Because I would rather be with my best friend at Camp Shalom than at Circle M without her. At least, I was pretty sure. It wasn't like it mattered anyway, since I would never have to make that choice.

"Bea? Please don't hate me."

I sighed. "I don't hate you."

But I did a little.

Frankie ran forward and almost knocked me down with her bear hug. "I knew you'd understand."

I mostly didn't. But part of being a best friend means faking it sometimes. And I still had the rest of the school year to get through, and I did not want to do it without my best friend. So I hugged her back, even though, deep down, I didn't want to.

A car honked. "Oh, right," Frankie said, smacking her forehead. "Mom's waiting. Want to go to the mall?" she asked, like the whole camp thing had never happened.

I poked my head out the front door and waved at Frankie's mom. "I guess…"

Frankie started to vibrate with excitement. "Now that I'm going to Circle M, I need all sorts of new things. Like a helmet and boots and *jodhpurs*. Do you even know what jodhpurs *are*?"

"Riding pants," I said, not catching Frankie's shopping enthusiasm.

"Of course! Riding pants! Oh, I'm so glad you're not mad at me, Bea. I couldn't deal if you hated me because I'm going to horse camp."

Speaking of not being able to deal. "I can't go to the mall," I blurted out.

Her face fell. "What? Why not?"

I scratched the back of my head. "I forgot…I… uh…I have to go with my mom to the drugstore." It wasn't a total lie. Mom had said we'd have to go shopping to get camp supplies. Probably not today, but it could happen. I glanced over my shoulder. Thankfully she was still in the shower.

"What for?" Frankie asked.

Good question, Bea. What for? "Uh… maxi pads. You know, what my mom calls *feminine hygiene products,*" I used air quotes and my deep announcer voice.

Frankie screwed up her face. "She needs your help buying maxi pads?"

"No." I rolled my eyes. "Of course not. But we're going to buy some *supplies* for me in case… *you know.*"

Frankie's eyes went wide in understanding. "Right…in case you get IT over the summer."

"Yeah, and it's one of those mother-slash-daughter bonding things she wants to do with me today. You know how it is." I gave another eye roll for believability.

She nodded, totally buying it. "Yeah, when I got mine, my mom got all weepy and weird. Who knew *becoming a woman* put so much pressure on mothers?"

Right. Her getting her period was just one more thing Frankie got to do first. Though to hear her complain about it, I wasn't missing much.

The horn honked again. "I'd better go." She leaned forward and gave me another hug. "I'll text you later to show you everything I got."

"Great," I said, trying to sound sincere. Frankie waved and bounded away from my porch. I closed the door and leaned against it.

"This summer is going to stink so bad," I said out loud.

Just then Dad came around the corner in his pajama bottoms and Metallica T-shirt, his bare feet slapping loudly against the tile. "What's that?"

I sighed. "I said that this summer is going to stink."

His forehead creased into three lines. "I wish you could be a bit more positive, Bea."

"Okay, how's this? I'm *positive* this summer is going to stink."

Dad rolled his eyes and turned toward the kitchen. "Come on. I need coffee. Talk to me in the kitchen."

I reluctantly followed. "Maybe I'll skip camp this summer."

"Not an option," he said as he reached into the cupboard for a mug.

"Why not? Maybe I could work with you for the summer?" Hanging out with Dad as he wired new houses for electricity wouldn't be so bad, right?

Dad put the mug down on the counter and turned to me. "A, you're eleven—"

"Almost twelve!" I interrupted.

I didn't think he even heard me. "—which means legally you're not even allowed to work, and I'm not insured for having kids on job sites. B, you'd be bored to tears, and C, I'm not losing the deposit we spent on Camp Shalom. So guess what, Queen Bea?"

"I'm going to Camp Shalom."

He nodded and reached for the coffeepot. "You're going to Camp Shalom."

And that was that.

FOUR

The rest of the school year was totally
awkward.

Frankie was getting ready to go to Circle M,
and I was getting ready to go to plain old
non-horse Camp Shalom. She (sort of) tried not
to talk about Circle M, but it was obvious she
was super excited. I couldn't really blame her.
I just wished she didn't have to be so super
excited around *me*.

Sometimes she'd say stuff like, "Oh, I wonder
what my horse's name will be," and I'd try to
change the subject, but then she'd get all dreamy-
eyed and continue anyway. "I wonder if he'll be

black with a star like Black Beauty or a pretty brown one like Seabiscuit. Hmmm."

At first I tried not to say anything in response, or I would talk about all the cool things that would be happening at Camp Shalom, but Frankie and the rest of our friends only wanted to talk about horses. No one cares about anything else when horses are involved.

Sigh.

Anyway, I was happy when school was finally over and Frankie and I had said our goodbyes. Sure, I was going to miss my best friend, and the tears I shed were real, but I was definitely not going to miss all the horse talk.

At least all the awkwardness was over.

Or so I thought.

On the Saturday before I was set to leave for Camp Shalom, Mom took me to the mall for that whole mother-daughter bonding thing. After she bought me two new bathing suits, we stopped at the food court for ice cream. I got a cone of Rocky Road, and she got a cup of French vanilla with salted caramel sauce. She even let me have a taste when I commented that it looked really good.

Then, as we were sitting there eating our ice cream in the noisy food court, she said my name in between spoonfuls.

I took another lick. "Uh-huh?"

"Bea," she said again, making me look over at her.

"Yeah?"

"You're going away soon."

Duh. "Yeah?"

"When we're done here, we'll go to the drugstore, and we can get you some *feminine hygiene products* for you to take with you."

"Okay. Thanks," I said, returning to my ice cream so she wouldn't go on like this was some sort of big deal.

She wiped her mouth with her napkin and reached for my hand. "Just in case, honey," she said, giving my fingers a squeeze. "I don't want you to not have anything with you, should it happen and you need it. I know the camp has supplies, but if it does happen, I don't want you to be afraid, and if you have your own things, you'll feel more comfortable and won't have to go to the infirmary."

Ugh. There was absolutely no reason for us to be having this conversation—couldn't she have simply slipped some stuff into my bag and been done with it?

"Yes, Mom. I get it. Thanks."

"Because when a girl becomes a woman, her body changes."

OMG. Please stop talking. But she was on a roll. When she got like this, it was best just to go with it. Eventually she'd wind down. At least this time I had ice cream to focus on.

"Maybe we should have gotten you a bathing suit with cups because your breasts are going to grow—"

"Hi, Mrs. Gelman. Hi, Bea."

I looked up.

OMG times a thousand, it was Jeremy, Frankie's way cute fourteen-year-old brother. Her way cute brother who was also going to Camp Shalom as a CIT, a counselor-in-training.

And there he was, standing right in front of us, interrupting my mother's talk about PERIODS and GROWING BREASTS.

I was going to die right there.

At least Mom had finally stopped talking. She smiled at Jeremy, somehow not horrified that he'd probably overheard her telling me about CHANGING BODIES.

"All ready for camp?" Mom asked.

Jeremy nodded. "Almost. I'm just picking up a couple of things. Sunscreen and stuff."

Mom looked around. "Where are your parents?"

"My mom dropped me off on her way to yoga."

"Oh, well, you're old enough to do your own shopping, I guess," Mom said. "But we can drive you home if you like. We just have one more stop at the drugstore, and it sounds like you're going there anyway."

You know how they say your life flashes in front of your eyes when you are about to get in an accident or something? Well, that happened to me in that second. Only it wasn't my life flashing in front of my eyes, but a mental picture of me holding a box of maxi pads while Jeremy stood there, pointing at the box and laughing. At me. And my CHANGING BODY.

My face was so hot it was basically on fire.

"MOM!" I shrieked, louder and much higher than I'd intended. But it was a dire situation. "I'm sure Jeremy can find his own way home," I managed to choke out.

The way Jeremy looked at me, it was obvious he thought I was a lunatic, but scaring him away wasn't such a bad thing in that second. And whether

I had or the universe was just handing me a silver lining, Jeremy shook his head and told my mother thanks, but he was meeting up with some friends and they'd take a bus home.

Whew.

My very clueless mom nodded and smiled at Jeremy, who said a polite goodbye and added, "See ya at camp, Beatrice," as he walked away.

Disaster averted, I finally exhaled.

"He's a nice boy," Mom said.

I didn't say anything but returned to my melting ice cream. But secretly I agreed. He *was* a nice boy. AND a very cute one who was nowhere near as gross as Frankie always made him out to be.

"Bea?" Mom asked, a weird tone in her voice.

"Yeah?"

She was frowning and staring at me hard.

"What?" I wiped my face with my napkin. She looked more concerned than she should have been about a blob of ice cream. "What is it?"

"Your face. You look like you've broken out in hives!"

"What?" I touched my cheek with the hand not holding ice cream. My face had felt hot, but I'd thought it was because of the extreme embarrassment from the moment before.

"Is your breathing okay?"

"Breathing? Yeah. What's happening?"

"Come on," she said, taking the cone out of my hand and getting up. "Let's go to the drugstore and get the pharmacist to look at you. I'm sure you're fine, but just in case."

"Wait, I'm not done," I said, reaching for my ice cream.

Too late. She'd dropped it in the garbage bin.

Ugh! Mothers.

It turned out I *was* fine. The pharmacist said since I didn't have any allergies, it probably wasn't from the ice cream but that maybe I had touched something and then my face. He showed Mom what kind of skin cream to buy, in case the hives didn't go away on their own.

We were relieved to hear I was going to be okay and that hives aren't usually a big deal.

Oh yeah, and then we bought feminine hygiene products, which was awesome.

Not.

FIVE

The day finally arrived for me to leave for my very first sleepover summer camp experience.

Alone. Frankie had left for Circle M a few days before. Not that I wanted to think about her. And how she had betrayed me.

I walked into the huge gym at the Jewish Community Center and had to stop at the doorway to take it all in. The room was crowded with kids of all ages, right up to teenagers. And their luggage. Lots and lots of luggage. Army-green duffel bags, superhero-themed hard-sided cases, pink backpacks with cute kitty logos, black wheeled bags. You name it, it was there. And the noise in the room was made louder by the echoes of a thousand people talking all at once.

It was a bit overwhelming. No. It was *a lot* overwhelming.

"Go on in, Bea," Mom said, giving me a nudge from behind. "We're already late."

Before I could even figure out where to go, a voice boomed through a megaphone. "All right, Camp Shalom campers! Two minutes until we start loading the buses. Cabins one through fourteen are first up through the east doors. Moms and dads, brothers, sisters, bubbies and zaidies, please start saying your goodbyes."

"Over here," Mom said, pointing to a big sign that hung on the wall. A bunch of girls about my age were standing under it, their assorted luggage scattered around their feet. We'd been told in advance that I'd be in Cabin 17 and that we needed to tag my luggage accordingly. It now made perfect sense why.

Cabin 17—my new family for the next four weeks. I quickly scanned faces for a friendly one. Most of the kids were talking to their assorted family members, but there was one girl, with a mass of curly red hair, standing on her own, gripping the handle of her plain black suitcase like it was her most prized possession—or maybe her security blanket. She looked terrified. And alone. Boy, did I know *that* feeling. Or, at least, I was going to in about two minutes.

I moved over and stood near her. She gave me a smile, but it didn't look like a real smile. It looked more like she was about to throw up. I hoped not. It was going to be a long bus ride, and I did not want to sit near someone who was likely to barf. Because, as everyone knows, barfing is totally contagious, and if I heard, saw or smelled barf, I was going to throw up too.

"So," Dad said loudly over the millions of voices. "This is it, huh?"

Mom just nodded and kept blinking.

"Give your dad a hug," he said, leaning down.

"Dad, you're going to suffocate me," I squeaked when he squeezed me too hard.

"Sorry, but I'm going to miss my Queen Bea. Promise me you'll write every day." By the time he got to "day," his voice was almost a whisper.

"Oh, Dad," I said. But it was hard not to choke up when *he* was *totally* choking up. "Every day? Seriously?"

"Fine," he said, clearing his throat. "Twice a week. At least!"

"Oh, all right," I said with a big sigh. "Since you'll miss me SO MUCH."

Anyway, we had to write home at least twice a week. The rules said they had to write, too, which I was glad of, especially right then when it suddenly felt really hard to say goodbye.

I let Dad go and nodded before I turned to Mom. She was an even bigger mess, with glossy eyes and a quivering frown. She hugged me hard too and said, "I'm going to miss you. But I know you're going to have a wonderful time and make lots of friends."

I nodded, though I didn't really believe I'd be making any friends, let alone lots of them. But Mom was already stressed, so I didn't say anything.

"Say bye to Stevie for me." I wasn't sure why I said that. My brother hadn't even bothered to get out of the car. He was too busy playing some game on his phone. At least he had a phone; I had to leave mine at home: no phones allowed at camp.

The megaphone boomed. "Cabins fifteen through twenty-nine now boarding the buses through the east doors."

"I guess this is it," Dad said again. And then he hugged me *again*, whispering in my ear, "You'll do great, Queen Bea. I know it. Just look for the silver lining. It's there—I promise."

"Thanks, Dad."

"We'll help you get your stuff onto the bus," he said.

I noticed some parents leaving. I took a deep breath and shook my head. "I think I'm okay. You guys can go."

Mom and Dad looked at each other and then at me.

"Are you sure, Bea?" Mom asked.

"Yeah. I can handle it." And really, the last thing I needed was to start my camp experience all teary. And the parents were *totally* getting teary. Best to make a clean exit before it got ugly.

Mom nodded. Dad put his arm around her shoulders and gave her a squeeze. "Okay. Be good. Write us when you get settled in."

I nodded, scared that if I tried to say anything, my throat would close up and all I'd be able to do was squeak. With another deep breath to prepare myself, I grabbed the handle of my suitcase. I gave my parents one last wave and then turned toward the east doors, falling in line with my fellow Camp Shalom campers.

No looking back. No matter how much I wanted to.

No looking back.

I kept my eyes forward. The girl with the red hair was in front of me, her curls bouncing with each step she took. I kind of wanted to pull on one—not to hurt her or anything, but to watch it bounce back into place. I wondered if the curls were natural or if she wore curlers to bed or something.

Suddenly, like she could tell I was staring, she turned around and looked at me.

She gave me another one of her smiles. This one was a little brighter. Maybe she wasn't going to barf after all.

I gave her a smile back.

"Hi," she said.

I took a breath, trying to calm the fluttery nerves in my belly. "Hi. I'm Bea. I'm in cabin 17 too."

"Bee? Like the insect?" she said in a strange accent.

"No, Bea as in short for Beatrice, but I hate being called Beatrice, so just Bea." I scratched at an itch on my neck.

Her lips formed an O. "Right. I'm Regan." She said it like *Reeegin*.

"Nice to meet you, Regan," I said as we shuffled forward in the line. But now she was beside me instead of in front of me.

"Likewise."

"Where are you from?"

"Ireland."

Wow. "This is a long way to come for summer camp."

She shrugged. "Mam sent me over for the summer. She said it would be good for me to make some friends, seeing as I spend all my time on the farm by myself. It was either that or muck out stalls all summer."

I stopped in my tracks, even though it made the girl behind me bump into my suitcase.

"Wait." I had to skip to catch up to Regan. "Muck out stalls?"

She looked over and frowned. "You know, in the barn."

Well, I don't have a barn, I was going to point out, but I didn't want to be mean. Maybe things were different in Ireland. Maybe everyone had a barn there.

"So, like, *horse* stalls?"

"Yeah, of course."

Wow. This girl gave up spending her summer with horses to come to a camp in a whole different country where she didn't know anyone. And there were zero horses. So weird.

I had to ask. "Don't you like horses?"

By this time the line had moved outside into the sun. Regan reached into her bag and pulled out a baseball cap, tugging it on over her curls. "Sure,

43

I like horses, especially my pony, Taffy, but a summer not having to work?" She shrugged again like she didn't need to bother saying anything else.

My first thought was, She has her own pony! My second was, I didn't realize horses were *work*.

"What does it mean to 'muck out stalls'?"

"You're a city girl, I gather?" she asked me, smiling so it didn't sound mean.

I nodded.

"Mucking out stalls is cleaning up all the horse poop and the dirty straw they pee on. It stinks, and it's heavy. Sometimes the dusty straw makes me sneeze too. Ugh, I hate mucking. Awful work, that."

I wondered if Frankie would have to muck out stalls at horse camp. I kind of hoped so.

"So why did your family send you so far away?"

"Mam's from here and came to this camp when she was a kid. But then when she grew up, she married Da, and they moved to Ireland because he got a job there. My grandparents still live here, and they wanted me to come here to meet some Jewish kids. There's not a lot where I'm from."

For being from opposite sides of the world, we seemed already to have a lot in common. "My parents want me to hang out with Jewish kids too," I said. "Especially because I have my bat mitzvah next year. Have you had yours yet?"

Regan shook her head. "No. But Da's not Jewish, so he doesn't see the big deal. Mam's working on him though." She shrugged. "My parents are coming here at the end of summer to pick me up, and then we'll go visit my grandparents before we go back home. I bet they'll work on him too. They really want me to have a bat mitzvah," she added, rolling her eyes.

I smiled, knowing what grandparents could be like. "So you came all the way here on a plane by yourself?"

She nodded. I was so impressed. She seemed so...I don't know...*grown up* to have traveled so far on her own.

We finally reached the bus. "Want to sit together?" I asked as we hefted our bags into the luggage compartment between the giant wheels. Some of the other kids' parents were helping them, but me and Regan had to do it ourselves. I felt kind of proud of that.

She looked at me, a bit confused. "I thought we'd already settled that when we became friends just now."

My stomach did a little flip of happiness. "Yeah. Uh, I was just making sure," I said as I followed her up the stairs onto the bus.

Maybe making friends isn't as hard as I thought.

SIX

The bus ride to Camp Shalom was actually quite fun. Mom had told me it would be over two hours, and I'd been dreading it, but with a new friend sitting beside me, the time seemed to rush by like the scenery outside the windows.

Regan told me what it was like living on a farm in Ireland and about her pony, Saltwater Taffy—Taffy for short. She also had two dogs, Winnie and Lady, two super-smart black-and-white border collies. Although she said they weren't exactly pets because they spent all their time protecting their flock of sheep.

It all sounded very cool to me but was nothing special to Regan, who lived it every day.

We had just decided that I would take the top bunk and Regan the bottom (she was afraid of heights, and I was afraid of being crushed to death, so it worked out perfectly) when the bus turned onto a gravel road. After a long, bumpy ride, we arrived at the entrance to the camp marked by a giant arch made from stone and wooden beams.

I was nervous, but having already made a friend, I was feeling excited too. Kind of how I'd felt when it was going to be me and Frankie. It wasn't going to be as cool as horse camp, of course, even though I had a better idea now of how much work horses would be, but maybe Mom and Dad were right. Maybe I *would* have fun.

The bus stopped, and the driver told us to stay in our seats.

Regan and I looked at each other and laughed because we were both already standing up. We sat back down.

The bus door opened and a woman came up the steps. She was wearing a T-shirt that said *DIRECTOR.*

"Welcome to Camp Shalom!" she said very loudly. "I'm Jamie Beth and before we get started, I need to ask you all a very important question." She looked around at all of us. "Are you ready to have a great summer?"

Everyone on the bus said, "Yes!" Even me.

But the director frowned and cupped her ear. "What's that?" she said. "I asked if you were all ready to have a GREAT SUMMER!"

Which made everyone erupt into super-loud cheering. I wanted to cover my ears. But it was still pretty fun to have everyone yelling like that. And it was easy to get caught up in the excitement.

"That's better!" Jamie Beth hollered. "Okay, kids, grab your bags. Any luggage that you put in the storage compartment under the bus will get taken to your cabin by this afternoon. Go find your cabin groups. You have half an hour to get settled, and then I'll see you in the mess hall. Got it?"

"What's a mess hall?" Regan asked me.

I shrugged. "Maybe that's where we do arts and crafts—that's always messy. Especially when you use glitter."

She nodded. "Right."

We started to file off the bus. We were almost at the back, so it seemed to take FOREVER. When I finally stepped down onto the gravel of the Camp Shalom parking lot, the first thing I noticed was the smell. I breathed in deeply. Camp Shalom was in the middle of a pine forest, and the air smelled like the live version of those tree-shaped air fresheners Dad hangs in the car. But times, like, about a thousand. And nicer too—much less likely to make me sneeze.

I was hoping to catch a glimpse of Jeremy, who had been on a different bus. But there were so many people in the parking lot that unless he were right in front of me, I'd never see him.

I took another breath and looked around. At first we seemed like just a huge, unorganized crowd of noisy people, but then I quickly realized we were all slowly being herded into our cabin groups.

"Over there," I said to Regan, pointing at a woman holding up a big sign with the number 17 on it. We made our way over to her. She was smiling and had pretty blue eyes and brown hair pulled back into a ponytail. She was wearing a Camp Shalom shirt that said *COUNSELOR*. Next to her, in an identical shirt, was a woman holding a clipboard. She had the same ponytail but her hair was lighter.

Regan walked right up to them and told them her name.

"Great to meet you, Regan," said the clipboard lady. "I'm Julie." She crossed Regan's name off the list. Then she turned to me. "And you are?"

My face got hot as she looked at me. I don't know why. I mean, she seemed nice and everything.

But the place was so noisy, and I didn't know her, and this was all so new, and with the exception of Regan, who I'd just met, I didn't know *anyone.* I was feeling really nervous again.

When I realized she was still waiting for my answer, I blurted out, "Bea."

Julie scanned the names on her list. "Beatrice?"

I sighed. Frankie wasn't here, so I'd have to correct them myself. "Yes, Beatrice. But please call me Bea. *Just* Bea."

"Got it. Thanks, Bea." She made a note on the clipboard. "Okay. I think that's everyone except…" She checked the list again. "Samantha and Carla. We'll just wait a few more minutes for them. They must have driven up with their parents."

While we waited, I looked around some more. Beyond the parking lot were a whole bunch of tall trees, and between them I could see buildings, and lots of kids and grown-ups with the same Camp Shalom shirts on. Everyone was moving about, but they were mostly in groups now. That was kind of a relief. If everyone stuck together like this all the time, I could be less afraid of getting lost in the woods.

There were several buildings off to the right that looked more like cozy cottages than the big cabins I'd seen in the brochure—they had cars in front, and one had a clothesline out back, bright T-shirts and shorts fluttering in the breeze. I wondered if the clothes would smell like pine trees too, but then, it wasn't like you could escape the smell out here anyway, so who would even notice?

There was a sign in front of the cottages that I could just barely make out. *Out-of-Bounds—NO Campers.* I was about to ask Regan who she thought might live there when I caught a movement out of the corner of my eye.

A little boy in a ball cap, maybe five or six years old, was hiding behind the tree with the clothesline tied to it. He seemed fascinated by all the commotion of campers getting into their cabin groups.

It was hard to see his face from so far away, but he was obviously shy, peeking out from the tree like that. I smiled. Maybe he found the first day of camp as overwhelming as I did.

"I'm Samantha," somebody behind me said, making me jump. "Samantha Beider."

Two girls were standing in front of Julie. "Hi, Samantha, welcome!" The counselor gave the other girl a big smile. "And you must be Carla?"

The girl scowled. "I'm Carly. Car*ly* with a *y*, not *Carla.*"

"Oh! Sorry about that, Car*ly*. Welcome!" Julie marked something down on her clipboard. "Great. Everyone's here now, so we can—"

Carly wasn't done talking though. "Samantha's dad drove us up so we wouldn't have to take *the bus*." She said it like riding on the bus was as bad as riding in the back of a garbage truck.

Regan looked at me, her eyebrows raised. I could tell she was thinking the exact same thing I was.

Samantha and Carly (with a *y*) were total snots.

It made me even more thankful that Regan and I were already friends and had worked out our sleeping arrangements.

"Okay, cabin 17," Julie said loudly over the crowd. "Follow us!" She and the other counselor, whose name, we learned, was Penny, turned and headed away from the parking lot, down a well-worn path into the woods.

Once we were all on the path, Julie called out, "I don't know, but I've been told!"

And then all the girls (except for me and Regan) repeated the line back to her. "I don't know, but I've been told!"

I couldn't believe that all the other girls knew what to do! I looked at Regan, and she shrugged. We kept marching behind the counselors.

"Cabin 17 is made of gold!" Julie hollered.

"CABIN 17 IS MADE OF GOLD!" Again the group repeated it back, even though it sounded kind of silly. But I nodded at Regan. It was just following along with a rhyme—we could do this.

"I don't know, but I've been told!" Julie sang out again even louder, which I hadn't thought was possible.

Regan and I joined in this time, belting out the words as we walked by the other cabins. "I DON'T KNOW, BUT I'VE BEEN TOLD!"

"Cabin 17 girls are too cool to behold!"

We all sang-laughed the line back to her. It was starting to look like camp without Frankie might just be okay after all.

SEVEN

Regan and I were the first ones through the cabin door, but before I even had a chance to take in what would be my home for the next four weeks, Carly pushed right past us. I was a camp newbie, so I had no idea what bunk was the best, but I had a feeling *she* did. And that she was set on grabbing it for her and Samantha. Typical.

Sure enough, she headed straight to the first bunk on the right, closest to the door, threw her bags on it, then waved at Samantha to join her. It made me think of how dogs pee on stuff to mark their territory.

"Okay, girls," Julie said loudly, causing all the

chatting in the room to cease. "Welcome to your home for the next few weeks."

I looked around at the cabin and counted five bunks on each side of the cabin; twenty beds total. At the back was a wall of huge cubby shelves that I figured were for our belongings. In the middle of the wall of cubbies was a smaller doorway that led to the very back of the cabin.

The cabin was brighter than I had expected, thanks to all the windows, and I already knew there was a bathroom in it somewhere, probably through that rear doorway.

"Girls, I'd like you all to meet Shira," Julie said, nodding her head toward the back of the cabin. Another counselor had appeared in the doorway.

"Shira's from Israel. She'll be teaching us some interesting things about Israel, and maybe even some Hebrew."

Shira smiled and waved at us. "Shalom, everyone," she said. "I also specialize in teva—nature and outdoors—so we'll be doing some hikes and cookouts."

"Ugh, outdoors," Carly muttered.

I glanced at Regan, and we rolled our eyes together. If Carly didn't like the outdoors, seriously, what was she doing at *camp*?

"So," Julie continued, "back there are the toilet and sinks. You will shower at the bathhouse we passed on the way here. Along the back wall are cubbies for you to store your stuff. Beyond the bathroom is the counselor living area. That's off-limits to campers unless one of us invites you in. Got it?"

We all nodded. It wasn't rocket science.

"Good. Now claim your bunks, and then we'll head to the mess hall."

"Will we do arts and crafts there?" Regan asked.

I was eager for the answer—I was looking forward to arts and crafts. In the camp brochure, there'd been a picture of girls doing pottery at those cool wheels. At the Jewish Community Center, where I'd taken classes before, we'd made stuff with clay, but only grown-ups got to use the wheels. You can make way cooler stuff with the wheels, not the lumpy candy dishes that your grandmother tells you she loves but probably only puts out when you're coming over for a visit.

Julie shook her head. "No, we're going to have lunch."

Regan looked at me and then back at Julie. "So the mess hall isn't where you do arts and crafts?"

Carly snorted and muttered something under her breath.

"No, hon," Julie said with a smile. "We do arts and crafts in the arts and crafts cabin. We *eat* at the mess hall."

Carly rolled her eyes and let out a soft, "Duh."

I felt bad because I was the one who had told Regan what I thought the mess hall was for.

And now my new friend looked stupid for saying it out loud.

My face had started to burn from embarrassment, but I had to do *something*. Because what if Regan didn't want to bunk with me anymore? What would I do then? I looked around, but all the other girls had paired up and were claiming bunks while I stood there, mortified.

I opened my mouth to tell everyone that it had been my idea, but before I got the chance, Carly yelled, "Ew, what's going on with YOUR FACE?"

I looked around to see who she was talking about, then realized who she was staring and pointing at. Me.

Everyone else was staring at me too.

"What?" I squeaked out in horror. My face was even hotter, so hot it felt like tiny flames were bursting out of my cheeks and forehead.

"Gro-oss!" Carly said, drawing out the word.

"What?" I said again, turning to Regan. "What is it?"

Regan's eyes went wide. All the other girls were talking. Not to me, but *about* me.

"What is it? Please!" I begged.

Julie walked over to me and, without a word, took my arm and led me into the bathroom at the back of the cabin. She flicked on a light switch, and in the mirror above the sink I saw what all the fuss was about.

You know, for a normally very quiet girl, I can scream pretty loud.

EIGHT

"Did you touch any plants or anything between getting off the bus and now?" the nurse asked as she examined my face. Her name was Lisa, and she looked puzzled. I stared at the deep crease between her eyes.

I was in the camp's infirmary, sitting on a paper-lined examination table in a room that looked a lot like the one in my doctor's office back home. It had canisters of tongue depressors and cotton balls and a box of gloves on the counter and one of those look-in-your-ear things hanging on the wall. But here I didn't have to sit around in a waiting room full of crying babies. I got seen right away. That was nice, at least—a silver lining.

Nurse Lisa looked at me, and I realized she was waiting for an answer. I went over my arrival at camp in my head. "No, I don't think so. I just went straight to the cabin."

She crossed her arms. "What did you eat before this happened?"

"Nothing. I haven't eaten since I left home this morning." Which explained the empty-feeling roll in my stomach, but not the hives on my face.

Because apparently that's what I had. Hives. Or urticaria, which sounds a lot more official even though it's just a fancy word for hives.

And, less of a joke, *Bea* has *hives*. Get it?

Hilarious. Or it would be if *I* wasn't Bea, the girl with huge, ugly red blotches on her face.

Nurse Lisa turned and sat down on the stool in front of the computer in the corner, put in a password and started reading the screen. "Your file says you don't have any allergies. And you've only had this kind of reaction the one time before? You're sure?"

"Yes, I'm sure." At first, when she'd asked, I had actually forgotten about the other time at the mall. Maybe because then I hadn't seen the hideous blotches until after I got home, and the cream had already started working.

"Anything you can think of that might be the same as the other time?" she asked.

I shook my head. "I haven't had any ice cream today," I said. *But oh boy, I could sure go for some Rocky Road right now.*

She typed something on the keyboard and turned to me. "I'm going to give you an antihistamine, and that should help. Have you taken antihistamines before?"

I shrugged. "I don't know. Last time, I just got cream."

She looked back at the computer and typed something else. Then, with a nod, she unclipped a key ring from her jeans and unlocked a cabinet with one of the keys. She took out a bottle and opened it, shaking a pink pill into a tiny paper cup on the counter. She locked up the cabinet again before she turned to me and handed me the cup.

"Are you itchy?" she asked as she reached into a fridge and got out a mini bottle of water, which she opened and handed to me.

"Not itchy. Prickly." I put the pill on the back of my tongue and took a big swallow of water.

She nodded. "That antihistamine should help. And here." She handed me a tube of cream. "If your face gets itchy, dab this on the spots. If they get worse, come back and see me."

She gave me a smile that said she was done with me.

"That's it?" I asked.

Nurse Lisa nodded. "That's it. No surgery or X-rays required this time."

My stomach lurched, and not just because it was empty. "Surgery?"

She laughed. "I was kidding. You'll be fine."

"But we don't even know what caused it."

She stood up and shrugged. "Often these things just happen—it could have been anything. Like I said, if it happens again or gets worse, come back and we will try to figure it out. But I don't think it's anything life-threatening. Just a minor reaction."

It didn't feel minor when those girls were staring at me, I thought. But I jumped down from the exam table, ripping the paper off it with my butt. "Oops, sorry."

"No problem. We put fresh stuff out for every patient anyway." She tore away the rest of the paper and stuffed it in a garbage pail in the corner.

"Thanks for the pill and the cream, Nurse Lisa," I said, heading toward the door. My stomach growled VERY loudly.

"You don't have to call me *Nurse* Lisa," she said

with a laugh. "Just plain 'Lisa' is fine. And you're welcome, Bea. Now go get yourself some lunch."

As I walked down the hall to the front of the clinic, I noticed a kid in a baseball cap standing on a stepstool in front of a big supply cabinet. For a second I thought he was stealing stuff. Then I realized he was filling the cabinet with supplies— boxes of gauze pads and bandages, that sort of thing.

He looked over at me as I got close.

"Hi," he said, smiling.

It was the same kid I'd seen by the cottages near the parking lot. "Hi," I replied. I tried not to stare, but it wasn't easy. He looked a bit odd—small and pale, with a big head. And somehow I knew he wasn't five or six.

"Just doing my job," he said in a really high voice.

"You work here?" I asked, surprised. Maybe he wasn't six, but I still didn't think he was a grown-up.

He laughed. "I don't stock supply cupboards

just for fun," he said, but the way he said it, I had a feeling maybe he *was* doing it for fun.

"Well, you're doing a good job. Keep up the great work."

"Thanks!"

I walked on past him, wondering why he wasn't outside with the rest of the campers.

Julie was still in the waiting room, which had gotten busier since I'd gone in to see Lisa. A couple of kids waited in the chairs now, one holding a blood-speckled tissue against his nose and another just sitting there, looking a bit angry. There were two counselors with them (their shirts gave them away). It was a rule that a counselor had to come with you to the infirmary.

Like when your face was all blotchy for absolutely no reason at all.

Julie jumped up out of her chair when she saw me. "You okay?" she asked. Even though I'd only just arrived at camp, I already knew she was my favorite counselor—on the way over she had tried to make me feel better by putting her arm around me and telling me it wasn't so horrible.

It was a lie, but I appreciated it just the same.

I nodded, trying to play it cool. "Just an allergic reaction."

"To what?" she asked.

I shrugged. "She didn't know but said that it happens sometimes. If it gets worse, I have to come back. But she gave me a pill and some cream. I'm good," I said as if I hadn't screamed in terror at my own reflection only a half an hour earlier.

Julie nodded. "Okay. Are you allowed to eat?"

"Yeah, she told me to go have lunch."

"Good. We'll join the rest of the cabin at the mess hall," she said, holding the door open for me.

My heart fluttered at the thought of meeting up with the girls again. I wished I'd asked the nurse how long before the medicine started to work. The last thing I needed was anyone to see me while I still had ugly splotches all over my face.

But I was really hungry, and I didn't have any snacks back at the cabin. Mom had given me money to buy stuff at the tuckshop (I still had no idea what tuck was; it didn't sound at all delicious), but obviously I hadn't had a chance yet. I didn't even know which bunk was mine! I hoped Regan had claimed a good one for us, but I'd have to wait until I talked to her to find out.

As Julie and I walked toward a big log building, I could hear what had to be a ton of kids inside— they were so loud, I could hear their voices outside, and the building was huge. "Is the whole camp in there?"

Julie smiled. "Pretty much. It gets like this most mealtimes."

I swallowed, and my face prickled. I stopped walking, not so sure I wanted to go in there. It suddenly felt very overwhelming. Even if Frankie was here, I wasn't sure I'd want to go in there.

"You okay?" Julie asked. "Aren't you hungry?"

I looked up at her. "Yeah, it's just…how bad is my face?"

Julie frowned and opened her mouth to answer just as a kid came running up from the direction of the cabins and practically ran into me.

"Hey!" I said, forgetting for a moment that I was covered in hideous spots.

The kid stopped and looked at me. It took a moment for me to recognize him. It took the same amount of time for him to recognize me.

"Bea?"

No.

Freaking.

Way.

It was Jeremy.

"Bea? Are you okay?" he asked. "What's wrong with your face?"

I shrugged like it was no big deal. "Allergic reaction." I wanted to say the technical term the nurse had used, but I'd already forgotten it.

"You okay? It looks…"

Hideous?

"…gross," he finally said. Which was just as bad as hideous. Maybe worse because *he'd* said it.

Julie jumped in. "It's just hives. Not contagious or anything."

Jeremy looked like he didn't quite believe her. I wanted to die.

"It's not as bad as it looks," I said. "I just got some medicine from the infirmary."

"Like zit cream?"

Ugh. Really? "No. *Allergy* cream."

"Oh. That's good, I guess. Well, I should go," he said suddenly, looking toward the mess hall.

"Okay, see you around," I said, trying to be cool.

Then he smiled. My heart fluttered, and I remembered why I had such a big crush on him. Maybe he really *did* want to see me around!

The thought made me wish I had a friend standing next to me who could analyze that smile with me, to make sure I wasn't just imagining things. I mean, that's what best friends are supposed to help with. But I guess it would have been weird if it was Frankie, since she's Jeremy's sister. But Regan maybe…

"So who was *that*?" Julie asked. I could tell by the way she asked that she was teasing me.

I felt my face prickle again and hoped the spots weren't getting worse. "He's my best friend's brother," I explained. "She was supposed to be here with me, but she's at horse camp instead."

She nodded knowingly. "Don't worry, Bea, you'll have plenty of fun here."

"Well, so far it hasn't exactly been a barrel of laughs."

"It's not so bad," she said kindly.

"Yes it is," I argued. "It's horrible. So much for making friends."

Julie tilted her head to the side. "What are you talking about? I thought you'd already made friends with Regan."

I shrugged.

"Don't worry. The medicine will kick in soon. I'm sure you'll be fine. Now come on, let's go eat. This afternoon we're going to do archery, and tonight's program is going to be awesome. You'll get to meet the rest of the staff and hear about the different programs—the Maccabiah Games and the musical and everything else. You'll see. Soon you'll forget all about this."

I highly doubted it, but—wait. She'd said something that caught my attention. "There's a musical?"

She looked around and then leaned in close. "Well, I'm not supposed to say anything before tonight. But I'll let you in on the secret. We're doing *Annie* this year."

I gasped. "*Annie*? Really?"

She nodded as she reached for the door to the mess hall. "Yes, but don't say anything to anyone or let on that you know."

I made a big show of pretending to zip my lip, but I could barely contain my excitement. *Annie* was my ALL-TIME FAVORITE musical. Mom had bought me a DVD of the movie, saying it was *her* favorite when she was a kid. We'd watched it over and over, until I knew every single word to every song. Of course, I would never sing in public, but watching *Annie* was just about my favorite thing in the world. Besides horses, of course. Mom used to joke that if I kept watching it so much, one day I'd wake up with curly red hair and freckles.

Secretly I'd wished she was right.

The mess hall was super loud inside. Kids were everywhere, sitting at long tables or walking around, some with platters, some empty-handed.

It all seemed like an unorganized mess. Maybe *that's* why it was called the mess hall.

"We're over here," Julie said, leading me around tables and dodging kids.

"This is ridiculous," I said.

"You'll get used to it. We always sit at the same table, and everyone takes turns going up to get the food."

I looked around, and all of a sudden it made sense. Kids weren't just wandering around aimlessly. They were getting up from their tables, picking up full platters of food and bringing them back to their groups.

Then I saw Regan's bright red hair and the empty spot on the bench beside her, and my breath caught in my throat. She had saved me a seat!

She looked up at me and smiled. Maybe I hadn't ruined everything!

"We missed doing the hamotzi," Julie said. "But I assume you know it. Say it in your head, okay?"

I was only half listening because my eyes were still on Regan, but I muttered, "Sure." Of course I knew the blessing on the food, thanks to years of Hebrew school.

Regan nodded at the seat beside her, and I almost skipped over to her. "Hi," I said shyly.

"Hi. I saved you a seat. Are you all right then?" she asked in her charming accent.

I sat down and, for the first time, noticed how good it smelled in the mess hall. My stomach did a big, impatient lurch. "Yes. It was just some sort of allergic reaction."

"Oh. That happened to me once when Taffy knocked me off into a rosebush."

"What? You fell off your pony?"

Regan nodded, passing me a dish of mac and cheese that started me drooling. "Taffy gets in moods sometimes. He didn't want to do a jump, so he dumped me in the rosebush."

I had no idea ponies got in moods. I scooped

some of the macaroni onto the plate in front of me. "Did you get hurt?"

"Just the thorns and the itchy bumps. The bush broke my fall."

"Still, that's awful."

Regan laughed. "That's Taffy." She looked at my face. "But you're okay then?"

"Yeah. They gave me some medicine. Does it look really awful?"

She frowned. "I wouldn't say it's *really* awful. Maybe medium awful? It might not be as bad as it was."

"Oh, look, it's *Spotty*." A voice from down the table. I turned to see Carly and Samantha staring at me. Then they rolled their eyes so perfectly it looked like a synchronized-swimming routine. I wondered if they practiced that. They could go to the Snarky Girl Olympics with those kinds of skills.

I didn't want to make things worse, so I turned away from them and began to eat my lunch.

"Don't mind them," Regan said. "They're just *cabbages*."

I smiled at her calling them "cabbages." I liked that she told me not to mind them. It made it easier to ignore the girls, even though I heard them snickering. Okay, so I couldn't *exactly* ignore them, but at least I didn't feel like I was going to die from humiliation anymore.

"I'm sorry about before," I said.

"For what?" she asked.

"I was the one who said the mess hall was for arts and crafts."

Regan shrugged. "So? You didn't know."

I looked around, then leaned toward her and whispered, "They laughed at you."

She shrugged again. "So what? I don't care what they think."

"Really? You don't care?"

Regan looked at me, her fork halfway to her mouth. "No. Why should I?"

I didn't know what to say. But Regan wasn't waiting for an answer. She had gone back to eating.

I shoved my fork into the noodles. And then I remembered something.

"Hey, so do you like musicals?" I asked.

"I do," she said, smiling.

I knew there was a reason we got on so well.

"Did you know they have one here at Camp Shalom?"

"Like for the kids then?" When I nodded, she asked, "Will you be in it?"

I shook my head. "No! I could never be onstage. I just love to watch. Maybe I can help backstage or something though."

"Backstage is no fun. Don't you sing?"

I shivered at the thought. "Not in front of people!"

"Because you're awful at it?"

"No," I said, almost laughing. That wasn't the problem. In fact, although no one else had ever heard me except singing with others at temple or at someone's birthday, I was a pretty good singer. But there was no way I'd ever do it in public.

Ever.

"Then why not try out? You seem excited about it."

"I am excited, but I can't."

"But why?" Regan asked, confused.

I shrugged, not liking this conversation anymore. "What about you? Do you sing?"

"A little. I like to act too. It would be fun if we could be in it together, don't you think?"

I didn't reply. With her red curls and freckles, Regan would be perfect for Annie. And it *would* be fun to do the play with her. But no way could I perform in front of people. I mean, it would be cool, but no way.

"I wonder what musical it is," Regan said.

I couldn't let on that I knew it was *Annie*—I'd promised Julie. I just shrugged and shoveled more mac and cheese into my mouth.

NINE

"Who are you looking for?" Regan asked. It was way later and we were sitting on the floor in the big lodge, waiting for the evening program to begin. The lodge wasn't as big as the mess hall, but it was still pretty huge—huge enough to hold the whole camp. With all the kids filing in, it was really loud too.

My face prickled at Regan's question. Apparently it was obvious that I was looking for Jeremy. "No one," I said.

"Tell me," Regan insisted.

I sighed. "Okay, fine. I'm looking for Jeremy. He's my best…er…good friend's brother. I thought maybe he could sit with us. You know, because we know each other from home."

"What cabin is he in?"

I turned back to the door, scanning the faces of all the kids still coming in. "I don't know."

"You sweet on him?"

Now my face was *really* heating up. I shrugged. "No, he's just a friend."

"Uh-huh."

She was obviously onto me. "Okay, yes. I like him. He's really cute and nice." Well, *mostly* nice. He *had* called my hives gross. But *definitely* cute.

Regan blinked. "And does he like you?"

I took a breath. "I don't know. I mean, I know he likes me, but I don't know if he *likes* me likes me."

She nodded.

I was relieved that she knew what I meant. "Do *you* have a boyfriend?"

Regan's eyes went wide. "I just got here today!"

Laughing, I said, "No, I mean back home."

She smiled. "Oh, right then. No. I'd rather spend time with Taffy anyway."

"Even though he dumps you in the bushes?"

She laughed. "He doesn't do that all the time."

"And you have to scoop out his stall?"

"Muck out, and yes, I'd rather clean up his poop and dirty straw than deal with boys. At least, all the boys I know. Your Jeremy sounds lovely."

"Well, I don't know about lovely, but—" I stopped talking because suddenly there he was. Striding into the lodge, smiling and laughing with his friends.

Look at me! Notice me! Come sit with me! my brain yelled as I held my breath, waiting for him to see me.

"Which one is he?" Regan whispered into my ear.

"The one in the red sweatshirt," I said, not taking my eyes off him.

And then, just like in the movies, in super-slow motion, Jeremy turned his head and looked right at me. Right into my eyes.

A squeak escaped my mouth, and then, all on its own, my hand rose up and waved at him. He gave a half smile and nodded toward his friends. Then he turned and followed them to the back of the lodge.

"Oh," I said as all the air rushed out of my lungs.

"You didn't really think he would sit with you, did you?"

Feeling betrayed by her VERY mean question, I looked at Regan. "I thought he might."

"I don't mean it like that." She shook her head. "A boy will *always* sit with his lads. If he sat with you, his friends would tease him no end. It doesn't mean he doesn't like you."

Hope made me suddenly dizzy. "You think he likes me?"

"I don't know, do I? But if I saw you two together, I'd know in a flash."

For someone who only hung around with her

horse, she seemed to know a lot. "How do you know so much about boys?"

"I have brothers, cousins, me dad. So many boys around me back home. A girl can't get away from them!"

"So you're like an expert."

"I suppose I am, Bea. I'll know if he likes you by how he acts around you." She bumped my shoulder with hers. "But you're such a sweet girl that I'm sure he does like you."

"You mean *like* me like me?"

"Yes, Bea." She nodded, her curls bouncing. "*Like* you like you."

I could only hope she was right.

"Okay, I'll do it," Regan said as we walked from the lodge back to our cabin.

We'd all sung "Hatikvah"—Israel's national anthem—which, thankfully, I had learned at Hebrew school (it was finally paying off!) and watched the counselors perform a silly skit. Then they had announced we'd be doing *Annie* as the camp play.

I was SO EXCITED, I could barely contain it.

After the announcement, the counselors performed "It's the Hard-Knock Life," so all the kids who'd never heard of *Annie* (they must live on the moon or something) could get a taste of the awesomeness that is the best musical in the entire world.

So when Regan said she'd try out for *Annie*, and not just the play but the role of Annie, I couldn't help it—I clapped my hands in excitement. She would be perfect.

"Under one condition," Regan said in a voice that kind of scared me.

I abruptly stopped clapping. "What?"

"You have to try out. I want you to be in it too."

My heart stopped and then found its way into my throat. "I can't."

"Yes, you can."

I would die. "Regan, I can't do it."

"Then I won't either."

Looking in her face, I could tell she was serious.

"I guess we don't have to be in the play," I said.

Regan stopped walking and crossed her arms. "Don't be daft."

"I'm not being daft, Regan. I *can't* do it!"

"Yes, you can. What are you afraid of?"

Panic made my heart pound. "I don't know," I said. "I just can't do it."

"No one has ever died from an audition."

With no phones allowed at camp, there was no way I could confirm this for sure. But I knew what she was getting at. Maybe it was a silly fear, but I was at camp to have *fun*, not to do things that terrified me. I said so and started walking again toward the cabin. I didn't want to get in trouble for being late for lights-out. And I also didn't want to continue this conversation.

"Bea!" Regan caught up to me, even though I was walking really fast.

I didn't answer.

"Bea," she said again, grabbing my arm. "I didn't mean to upset you. But it wouldn't be any fun by myself. You don't have to do a big part or anything. Just be one of the orphans. I want us to do it *together*."

Her words sounded a lot like what I'd said to Frankie. That I wanted to go to camp *together*. Because friends do things *together*.

I swallowed hard, then looked at my new friend. "Okay," I said.

Her face lit up. "Really?"

"Really. But just something small." Maybe I could do the part of Molly, Annie's best friend.

Regan threw her arms around me. "We'll have so much fun! You can help me learn the songs. This will be the best play ever!"

It was hard not to catch her enthusiasm, even though just the thought of auditioning made me feel like I did at Rosh Hashanah last year when I had the flu and had to run away from the table to barf up my bubby's famous apple kugel.

So not good. Not good at all.

Later that night, once we'd climbed into our bunks, Shira came in and taught us an Israeli lullaby, "Numi, Numi." But even though it had a pretty melody, it did not help get me to sleep. Not one bit.

I listened to the creaks and groans of mattresses, and the breathing of many girls sleeping, and the whispers of Carly and Samantha, who were *supposed* to be asleep but were both in Carly's bunk talking about who knows what (probably my hideous spots). I thought about all that had happened in just one day at camp.

I was away from home for the first time. Without my parents or my best friend or even my annoying little brother. I'd already had to deal with hives and mean girls and had somehow been talked into auditioning for a play. And, if I was successful, I would have to get up onstage in front of the WHOLE ENTIRE CAMP. It was all too much.

Even though I was surrounded by a cabin full of girls, I felt very frightened and terribly alone.

This was what homesick felt like, I realized. And it really was like a sickness, because my body felt heavy and tired and sad, just like it had at Rosh Hashanah. Although I could have really gone for a big plate of my bubby's kugel right about now—warm and delicious and reminding me of home.

Lying there in my bunk, I couldn't find the silver lining, no matter how hard I tried.

TEN

I woke up to the drumming of rain on the cabin roof. At first it was a nice sound, a rhythmic, soothing thonk-tha-thonk, tha-thonk, tha-thonk that made me want to pull up the blanket and snuggle in.

But then Julie came in and turned on the lights, causing groans all over the room. I obviously wasn't the only one who wanted to stay in bed.

"Get up, girls!"

"But it's raining!" one girl moaned

"So?"

"We can't go out in the rain!" another camper whined.

"What if we get hit by lightning?" This from the other side of the cabin.

"We'll have to take that chance," Julie said in a voice that clearly meant *get your butts out of bed.*

"My parents will sue you if I get hit by lightning," said someone else who sounded a lot like Carly.

"I'll take that chance too. Come on, girls, you've got fifteen minutes to get dressed, or you'll miss breakfast."

Amid another chorus of moans, mattresses squeaked as we all started getting out of our beds. I climbed down from my bunk, ready to say good morning to Regan. But she was gone, and her bed was neatly made.

I looked around the cabin but didn't see her. Maybe she was in the bathroom.

I slid my feet into my slippers after doing a little hop—the cabin floor was FREEZING—and headed to the back of the cabin. Of course, there was a lineup for the bathroom since all the girls were getting up at the same time. While I waited, I checked in the mirror and was happy to see only a few spots remaining on my face, just faded little red dots.

The stuff the nurse had given me was obviously working, and I was relieved. Especially if I was going to be running into Jeremy—sort of accidentally on purpose.

"Looks better," Julie said after she spit her toothpaste into the sink. She was looking at me in the mirror too.

I nodded. "Yeah. Thanks. So what are we going to be doing today if it keeps raining?"

She turned off the tap and put her toothbrush into the plastic holder. "We'll skip swimming, but we've got arts and crafts, which is inside, and then probably do some indoor games at the lodge after lunch. Then there's free time so you can write letters home."

I made a face. Julie laughed. "You know the rules. You have to send two letters a week to your parents."

"I know," I said. "Or maybe we could practice for the *Annie* auditions?"

She smiled. "So you're trying out?"

I took a deep breath. "Yes. Both Regan and I are."

"That's great," Julie said. "It's so much fun putting on these productions. The parents really love it too."

Parents? My heart stopped. "Wait. What?"

Julie brushed her hair back and put it into a high ponytail as she said, "We perform the show for visitors' day. They said that last night—didn't you hear?"

I must have been talking to Regan when they'd mentioned the visitors'-day part.

That meant *even more* people, *grown-up* people, would be watching the production. My stomach objected to this brand-new information and started to roll around. Or maybe I was just hungry.

Either way, I didn't like the idea of performing in front of the whole camp *and* everyone's parents, especially mine!

Julie looked around, clapped her hands and said loudly, "Okay, girls, hurry it up. Ten minutes!"

Ahh! I hadn't even been to the bathroom yet. I had to get dressed. Otherwise I'd never be ready in time. I went and grabbed my clothes for the day and tried to find my rain poncho among the not-so-neatly folded clothes in my cubby.

"*You're* trying out for the play?" It was Carly, standing next to me as she pulled on her shorts.

She said it like I had a contagious disease or something.

"Yes," I said. Not the best comeback, but whatever.

"You won't get in. You're not musical material."

I had no idea what she meant by musical material, but it wasn't like I even *wanted* to do it anyway.

Huh.

That's when it occurred to me. She might be onto something. If I wasn't good enough at the audition, I wouldn't get in. But, of course, Regan *would*, and she'd have to do it without me. And then everything would work out exactly as I wanted— they'd give me a behind-the-scenes job, and Regan would be Annie. We'd be together but not.

It would be PERFECT.

"Maybe you're right," I said to Carly.

"What?"

"Maybe I'm *not* musical material."

She stared at me and blinked several times. Maybe she'd expected me to argue with her. She humphed and walked away.

The morning was taken up by arts and crafts, or, as we were now calling it, A&C. We had to choose to make either friendship bracelets or beeswax Shabbat candles. I kind of wanted to make the candles, but

Regan suggested we make bracelets for each other. That sounded like a good idea, because then we'd each have something from the other, officially bonding us together as friends.

I liked that. And maybe, if I got good at making them, I'd take one home to Frankie. Maybe.

So far, though, I wasn't very good at it. Abby, the A&C instructor, started mine off after I'd picked out colors I thought Regan would like—greens and purples. She gave me good directions, and I got to take it with me so I could work on it during free time. I even had a big safety pin to hold it in place while I braided it. I just needed some practice getting the knots tight enough. I hoped Regan wasn't too fussy about it being perfect. Because it was definitely not going to be that.

Regan had tried to hide mine from me, but I snuck a peek and saw that she'd picked orange, yellow and blue, and I was happy with that—the bracelet would be really colorful and would look nice on my wrist.

So even though it was pouring rain outside, we had a good morning, and I almost couldn't believe it when Julie showed up to tell us it was time to go to lunch.

After we'd eaten hot dogs and salad (I had to quietly remind Regan why there was no cheese to put on the hot dogs—she'd forgotten that Camp Shalom is kosher, which meant dairy and meat were never served together at a meal), we all scraped any leftovers on our plates into the big pail Julie called the "slop bucket." That was the perfect name, as the pail was totally disgusting by the time we were finished. Then we took our plates to the dish station. It was kind of like cleaning up at home, so it wasn't a big deal. But to hear Carly and Samantha complain, you'd think cleaning up after themselves was the worst thing ever.

"I wonder if they have maids at home," I whispered to Regan as we were getting ready to leave the mess hall.

"Probably." She leaned into me. "They're like twins with their matching mean-girl tiaras—they probably even have servants to polish them."

That made me giggle.

"What's so funny, Spotty?" Carly asked.

"Nothing," I said and then cursed myself for answering to that name. I should have just ignored her.

"Her name's *Bea*," said Regan in a very Frankie-like way.

Maybe Regan is another part of my silver lining.

"Oh right, like a bug," Carly said, her snark volume on full blast.

Even though Samantha laughed, I didn't feel too bad. Because please. Like I hadn't heard *that* before. Jeez, even my little brother came up with more original "bee" stuff. I was starting to get what

Regan meant about them being cabbages.

Regan rolled her eyes and looped her arm around mine. "Don't pay them any mind, Bea. They're just jealous."

I didn't know what Carly and Samantha had to be jealous of. I mean, it's not like I have a maid or a tiara. But it seemed to shut the girls up, so I let Regan lead me toward the door. I was about to flip up my hood in preparation for going out in the rain when I heard my name. Not *Spotty*, but my actual name.

I turned, and there was Jeremy. Standing right there.

Regan hummed a *mmhmmm* beside me.

"Hi, Jeremy," I said.

"Your face looks better," he said.

"Thanks. It feels better."

He smiled. I swear, I almost fainted right there.

"Hi," Regan said. "I'm Regan."

"Hi. I'm Jeremy. I know Bea from back home."

He gave my arm a nudge. "I'm almost like her big brother, right, *Beatrice*?"

My big brother? I looked at Regan, but she was looking at Jeremy. So then I looked at Jeremy. He was looking at Regan. Pretty, confident Regan with the cool accent and the red curls. *Oh no.*

"We need to go," I said, grabbing Regan's arm.

"Where are you off to in such a hurry?" Jeremy asked.

"We have to go practice for *Annie.*"

"Right," Regan said. "Auditions are tomorrow."

"You're going to be in the play?" Jeremy asked.

I nodded and said, "Yes," as if he was talking to me.

"Maybe I should try out," Jeremy said.

"You totally should!" I said without thinking. Jeremy was more of the sporty type—I'd never heard him say anything before about wanting to act or sing. But if it meant watching him onstage and getting to hang around with him and maybe helping him with costumes and stuff, it was all good. I forgot all about getting out of there.

"Yeah, it's going to be fun," Regan said. "And I know Bea would love to help you practice—she knows all the songs."

Jeremy looked at me with his eyebrows raised.

I lifted my chin proudly. "It's true. I know every word to every song."

"Impressive," he said, and I could tell he meant it, which made my stomach do a little flip that had nothing to do with the extra hot dog I'd had at lunch. I was about to ask him if he wanted to practice with us when another boy came up to him, bumping him with his shoulder.

"Hey, Ferstein, come on, it's time for Capture the Degel. Let's go."

Jeremy nodded at his friend. "I'm coming. Just talking to my baby sister's little friend."

Baby? Little?

"See you later, Bea. Bye, Regan, it was nice meeting you."

"Likewise," said Regan with a charming bob of her head. Did every single thing she did have to be so charming?

As soon as Jeremy was gone, I turned to Regan. "So?" A part of me was still holding out hope that she would say that OF COURSE Jeremy liked me. *Liked* me liked me.

Instead she frowned. "I don't know, Bea."

"What?" I squeaked, letting out the breath I was holding.

"He said you were almost like his little sister…"

I felt my heart lurch and fall into my stomach. "Yeah…" I'd been so hoping it didn't mean what I knew it probably meant.

Regan put her arm across my shoulders and led me out into the rain, which felt very fitting since I was feeling very dreary. But then she adjusted my hood so I wouldn't get soaked and said, "Don't you worry, Bea. We'll get him to like

you. You watch. He said he'd come to auditions—
we'll make you irresistible."

Which is the kind of thing a real friend would say.

ELEVEN

I tried to put Jeremy out of my head so we could practice for our auditions. Well, so *Regan* could practice, and I could figure out how to ruin any chance of being in the show as a performer.

We found a quiet spot in the forest. Julie had given us free time to do whatever we wanted, as long as we were back in time for yoga, so that gave us a full hour to practice. I felt a little guilty that I wasn't back at the cabin, writing a letter home, since I'd promised Mom and Dad I'd write right away, but this was more important. And anyway, I could write them a quick note later in bed, even if I had to do it under the covers with a flashlight after lights-out.

Thankfully, the rain had stopped, so we'd ditched our raingear, and although it was kind of damp and sloppy in the woods, we weren't getting too wet. Every once in a while, when the wind blew, leaves dripped on us, but we just ignored it.

We'd decided we would both sing the most famous *Annie* song, "Tomorrow." It was the one Regan knew best. I knew them all, of course, but it didn't matter.

Because when I sang I would be SO awful, they would have to give Regan the part of Annie and wouldn't dream of giving me *any* role. I felt bad for deceiving her, but she wouldn't accept that I really didn't want to be in the play, so this was the only way. She'd be in it and I wouldn't. *And* I'd be saved from dropping dead of stage fright. Basically, I was saving my life.

She sang the song first and I was impressed. She wasn't half bad, singing about how the sun would come out tomorrow. She had a nice voice and did a good job, so there wasn't much feedback for me to offer other than she should hold a few of the notes longer. And to try to not look so serious when she sang. Maybe she was just nervous. I got that.

Then it was my turn. I was terrified of singing in front of her, but I told myself I was *trying* to be a bad singer, so I didn't have to feel pressured to impress her. In fact, it was exactly the opposite. The *less* impressed she was, the better.

In fact, if there were a contest for who could sing THE WORST EVER, I would have won it that day for sure. I made my voice go up and down and breathed at all the wrong times—whatever I could do to make myself sound like an injured cat, I did.

And it worked. I sounded horrible, and *I knew* I sounded horrible. But I pretended I had NO IDEA.

Once I was done, Regan just stared at me, blinking. It was hard not to laugh or even smile at the look on her face. She was trying to come up with a nice way of telling me how awful I was.

Good luck with that.

"So?" I asked innocently.

"Er…"

"How did it sound? Do you think I'll get in?" *Hopefully not.*

"Maybe you could use a bit more practice," she said.

"Oh. Okay, well, yeah, I'm a bit rusty. It's been a while since I've sung. Maybe I'll try it again. But why don't we sing together?"

"That's a grand idea. We can help each other through the hard bits." Which I'm sure was her nice way of saying, "Follow my voice and maybe you'll get a bit better" or "If I sing too, maybe I'll drown you out."

What a good friend she is. Trying to help the worst singer in the world.

We worked through the song again. But despite all the "practice," I didn't get any better. Maybe I even got a little worse.

It started to rain again. It was time for us to get back anyway, so Regan suggested we pick it up later. The drizzle quickly turned to a downpour, heavy raindrops splashing down loudly onto the leaves and then onto us. We began to run toward the cabin.

Just then I stepped in some mud and my toe caught on a root that was sticking up. I went flying (and squealing) through the air.

I landed facedown in a huge puddle of mucky, disgusting sludge.

"Bea!" Regan yelled, grabbing my arm to haul me up. "You okay?"

I spit about a gallon of mud and gritty water out before I was able to speak. And then I spit a bunch more times because dirt tastes gross. Trust me.

"Ugh, look at you! C'mon, we need to get you back to the cabin."

I shook my head. My shorts were soaked through, and even my underwear was cold and soggy. "I need a shower and shouldn't track all this guck through the cabin," I said. "I'm going to go straight to the bathhouse—can you do me a favor and get my towel and shampoo and some clothes from my cubby?"

"Of course," Regan said and jogged off toward the cabin. I took my time getting to the bathhouse. It wasn't like I could get any wetter, so I just let the rain pelt down on me and wash off some of the dirt. I was on the verge of being uncomfortably cold, but a hot shower would fix me up quick.

Knowing Regan would be on her way soon, I peeled off the wet clothes and stepped into a shower stall, making the water as hot as I could take it. I stood under the warm, comforting spray and let it wash the last of the crud off me.

A few minutes later I heard Regan calling me.

"I'm over here," I said.

"Here you go." She handed me my shower caddy around the edge of the curtain. "Your clothes are on the bench here."

"Thanks," I said, putting the caddy on the ledge. "Did you tell Julie what happened?"

"Yeah. I have to go back, but she said not to worry. If we're not at the cabin, we'll be down at the lodge. I'll take your dirty clothes with me. Julie said if I hurry, we can drop them at the laundry on the way to the lodge."

I double washed my hair and used extra conditioner, rinsing an extra-long time to make sure all the grit was out, before I turned off the water. Reaching for my towel, I hummed a few bars from "Tomorrow," knowing I could sing it even better than Regan if I tried. Not that I didn't think Regan was a good singer. I just knew secretly that I was better.

As I dried off and got dressed in the clean clothes folded neatly on the bench, I was still humming a song from *Annie* but had moved on to "It's the Hard-Knock Life," my second-favorite song.

As I left the bathhouse with my towel in one

hand and my shower caddy in the other, I looked up at the clearing sky.

"The sun's coming out," I said aloud. I felt so much better after that shower. *Just like in the song. Silver lining.*

I was about halfway to the cabin when I heard my name. It took only a fraction of a second to recognize the voice.

Jeremy.

My heart raced as I slowly turned toward him, pasting a smile on my face and wondering what I would say to him. When had it gotten so awkward?

"What's going on?" he asked, nodding toward my full hands.

"I just had a shower. I fell in a puddle," I said, feeling my face suddenly prickle. I wondered if that puddle had been filled with poison-ivy soup.

"Oh," he said. "I was coming to see if I could practice with you and Regan for the auditions." He looked around. "Where is she?"

"We finished practicing," I said. "My cabin all went to the lodge."

His gaze moved over my shoulder. "Not all of them."

And before I could even turn around to see who was behind me, I got pushed from behind. Hard.

I was knocked off-balance and into Jeremy, causing him to let out an "Oof!" as my shower caddy rammed into his gut and then fell to the ground. My forehead hit something hard, and I grunted in pain.

Somehow we didn't fall down, but I soon realized it was because I had grabbed him to steady myself. When I realized I was still gripping his arms, I gasped and backed up, only to stumble and fall backward onto my butt.

It was only then that I heard the giggles behind me. I turned, and, as expected, there stood the Tiara Twins, Carly and Samantha, howling with laughter.

"What the…?" Jeremy muttered.

Samantha shrugged while Carly smugly said, "Spotty wanted to give you a kiss. I guess she lost her balance. She doesn't have a lot of practice with kissing, you know."

WHAT?

NO!!!!!

I turned back toward Jeremy, who was looking at me, wide-eyed in disbelief.

Wait. Did he believe them? "No, that's not…no, Jeremy, no!" was all I could get out.

Because the Tiara Twins had started chanting, "Spotty and Jeremy, sitting in a tree, k-i-s-s-i-n-g."

"NO, WE WEREN'T!" I hollered. But it was no use. The truth didn't matter, and they weren't listening anyway. They were too busy making kissing noises.

Then they began hooting like howler monkeys as they ran off into the woods, still chanting.

Which left me alone with Jeremy.

I couldn't. I just couldn't.

Without looking anywhere near him, especially as he said my name, I picked up my towel and
shower caddy and then ran for the cabin as fast as
I could, crying the whole way. I would never, ever
be able to face Jeremy again.

"I can't go," I said to Regan the next afternoon. I'd
gone to the infirmary in the morning with another
case of hives and had gotten more medicine from Lisa.
Then I'd moaned to Julie that I wasn't fit to do any
activities and had stayed cooped up in the cabin all
day. I'd even written a letter to my parents that basically said camp stunk and begged them to come and
get me. But then I'd ripped it up into teeny-tiny little
pieces and written them a "Hi! Camp is great…blah…
blah…blah" letter. Because the last thing I needed was
a lecture from Dad on silver linings. Please.

"You *have* to go," Regan said, sounding panicked.
"It's auditions tonight!"

"That's what I'm talking about! I can't show up there now!" I was lying on Regan's bunk (too distraught to climb up to my own) with my arm over my eyes, blocking out the world.

Although the world could surely still see that I had a face full of hives (again), so I wasn't hiding anything from anyone. Everywhere I turned, there I was. And boy, I was getting awfully tired of me.

Regan sat beside me on the edge of the bed, trying to be a good friend. "They're not that bad. You'll be fine soon."

I took my arm away from my face and looked at my friend. Didn't she get it?

"The hives are the *least* of my worries, Regan. Jeremy thinks I tried to kiss him! Do you under-stand what that means?"

"That he knows you're horrible at kissing?" Carly sneered from two bunks over. She spoke just quietly enough that the counselors wouldn't hear.

"You! Hush your mouth!" Regan barked. She

turned back to me. "I'm sure he doesn't truly think that," she assured me in a very soothing tone.

"Right," Carly said with a snort.

"I've had enough of you," Regan said as she stood up, her accent getting even thicker the angrier she got. "How would *you* feel if someone did that to you and the boy *you* were sweet on?"

"Regan!" I hissed. But it was too late. She didn't even realize what she'd done.

"Oh, *really*? So Spotty really *does* have a crush on that boy?" said Carly with a sneer. "I'd suspected as much, but now I know for sure. That's *even more* hilarious."

"I want to die," I moaned.

"No you don't," Regan said. Sure, it was easy for *her* to say. Jeremy didn't think *she* had tried to kiss-attack him before landing on her butt for her second time in one day.

"Now come on. We can practice on the way to the mess hall and then again after dinner."

I put my arm over my face again so I wouldn't have to look at her. "I'm not going. I would rather DIE. I'm going to stay in this cabin for the rest of the summer."

"Look," Regan said, exhaling loudly through her nostrils and sounding a lot like my mother right before she said something like, *I've had enough of this business, Beatrice Gelman.* "I know you're embarrassed, but I bet Jeremy was even more embarrassed."

I snorted. "*He* was even more embarrassed? I doubt that's possible."

"You have to go, Bea. And anyway, he probably won't even show up for auditions."

"Do you really think so?" I asked, still doubtful.

"I would bet money on it. Please—do it for me. It's really important to me."

She was my one friend here at Camp Shalom. Plus, she seemed really sure that Jeremy wouldn't be there…

"Fine, I'll go," I said at last.

Regan clapped her hands. I, on the other hand, couldn't think of even one thing worthy of applause.

TWELVE

After dinner we walked to the lodge, straggling behind the rest of the girls from our cabin, especially Carly and Samantha, so we could practice a bit more. I told Regan I didn't feel like singing and that she should go ahead.

She sounded even better now than she had in the forest. I told her so.

"Thanks. I'm a bit nervous. Are you?"

I spoke the absolute truth when I said, "I'm a lot more nervous about seeing Jeremy."

"I told you, I don't think he'll show up. Boys get embarrassed very easily. Like, when I got my period and my brothers found out? I thought Declan and

Kevin would tease me endlessly, but they kept away from me for a whole week. Like I was contagious. Talk about cabbages."

"Really? A whole week?" I wondered if that trick was going to work on my own brother when my time came. I sure hoped so. It would be like a superpower.

"Aye."

"But that's different. Those are your brothers. And this is about kissing—or I guess *not* kissing. Because I DID NOT try to kiss him."

"I know you didn't, Bea." She shook her head as we approached the path up the hill to the lodge. "But they're still lads, so it's the same."

I didn't believe her, but it was nice to think that maybe Jeremy would be scared off and leave me to concentrate on blowing the audition.

Ugh. I couldn't even think about it without totally blushing, which made my face feel even pricklier!

And then there was THAT. Please. Like I hadn't endured enough already? Before that day in the mall,

I had never had hives, and now, at camp, I was like the queen of hives. That's me, Queen Bea of Hives.

So not funny.

"How're the spots?" I asked Regan before we went in.

She stopped and scanned my face. Based on the look on *her* face, it didn't look good. "Improving," she said, not meeting my eyes.

"Still hideous. I get it."

"Not *hideous*. You're fine, Bea."

Right. It didn't matter anyway. In fact, maybe the hives would help keep me out of the show. Who wanted a spotty Pepper or Molly? Well, now that I thought about it, a spotty *Pepper* was kind of funny.

Maybe having hives right now wasn't such a bad thing after all. Silver lining.

"Let's get this over with," I said.

"Aren't you excited?" Regan asked.

Oh, right. I was supposed to be acting excited. "Yes, just a bit nervous is all."

She smiled. "Me too, but with all your excellent coaching, I think we'll both do great."

Don't count on it.

We stepped through the doors.

"Oh no," I whispered.

Regan followed my eyes to where I was looking. Jeremy.

"Oh," she said. "I really didn't think he'd come."

"You were wrong," I said, more harshly than I'd meant to. "Now what am I supposed to do?"

She looked at me and frowned. "Just pretend like it never happened."

"Right. Sure. That sounds easy."

But it *was* easy at first, because right after I made a Bea-line (I crack myself up) to the other side of the lodge, as far away from Jeremy as was physically possible, the drama counselor, Shawna, stood up on the stage and clapped her hands.

"Welcome to the *Annie* tryouts, everyone," she said in a strong voice. She probably wasn't too old—like, twenty or something. And it seemed like she'd had a lot of practice acting—she wasn't yelling, but she was definitely making herself heard. Julie had told me that most of the counselors were college students, so I wondered if Shawna was taking drama at school. That would be a cool degree to get. You know, for someone *not* prone to horrible stage fright. Or hives.

"If you're trying out for a lead role, please come over here," Shawna continued. She motioned to the right side of the stage. About fifteen kids, including Regan (after I gave her a little push) and Jeremy, made their way over. Pretending I wasn't looking at him, just in case he turned around, I watched Jeremy out of the corner of my eye. He was smiling as he spoke to Regan. She smiled back at him, and I suddenly wished I could hear what they were talking about. I didn't think Regan would say anything to him about the not-kissing incident, but I desperately hoped I was not the topic of conversation.

But then, as I watched them, it occurred to me that they seemed awfully friendly for people who'd only just met. And they were standing very close. Jeremy had a goofy look on his face—one I'd never seen before. That's when it hit me.

Jeremy likes her! As in, likes *her likes her.*

He's mine! Okay, not *actually* mine, but I had dibs, right? Regan didn't know him. Regan wasn't BFFs with his sister. Regan didn't even live in the same country! As I watched Regan giggle at him, I got a little angry. Okay, a lot angry.

Before I realized what I was doing, I'd walked over to them.

"Bea!" Regan said, obviously surprised given how I'd gone on about avoiding Jeremy at all costs.

"Hi, you two," I said, keeping my eyes on Regan. If I looked at Jeremy and he smirked or hinted at all about what had happened earlier, I would die on the spot.

"Hi," Jeremy said in kind of a weak voice. Before

I could stop my traitorous eyes, they glanced over at him, just long enough to see that his face was horribly red. Maybe Regan was right. Maybe he *was* embarrassed.

"What are you doing here?" Regan asked me.

"I changed my mind. I think I *will* try out for a lead."

My brain nearly exploded as it caught up to what my mouth had just blurted out.

I can't be in the play!

Regan's eyes went wide. "Which one? Not Annie?"

It wasn't like I'd given it a lot of thought. The idea had just occurred to me that very second. But I knew I couldn't try out for Annie against her. And anyway, it was way too big a part. "Maybe Miss Hannigan."

"Who's Miss Hannigan?" Jeremy asked.

Still unable to look him in the eye, I said, "She runs the orphanage."

"Orphanage?"

Now I actually looked at him. "Yes, the *or-pha-nage*. Like, where Annie comes from? You know this play is all about an orphan named Annie, right?"

His face got even redder. "Of course I know that!" But the way he said it sounded like he *hadn't*. What was he even doing trying out?

"Okay, everyone," Shawna said from the stage. "We'll start with Annie. Anyone trying out for her, come up to the stage now, please."

Even though I was not AT ALL happy about her sudden closeness with Jeremy, Regan was my friend, so I gave her a quick hug and whispered in her ear that I knew she'd do great. She squeezed me hard and then joined the others.

Samantha was up there, along with three girls who weren't from our cabin. She looked at me and rolled her eyes, so I stuck my tongue out at her. No, it wasn't a mature thing to do, but she was half of the reason I couldn't even look at Jeremy right now, even though he was standing right next to me.

"I hope she gets it," said Jeremy suddenly.

I jumped, not expecting him to talk to me. "Who? Samantha?"

"No. Regan."

"Why? Do you like her or something?" I blurted out—then quickly realized I definitely didn't want to hear his answer. "Never mind."

"Bea?" he said quietly.

I looked at him, and my entire face got hot and prickly. "Yeah?"

"Will you help me?"

"Help you how? Voice coaching? It's a little late for that. You're going to be auditioning soon." I looked around. "But you're probably going to get whatever part you want, since you're the only boy here. Daddy Warbucks is the only lead, so that's the one you want, and unless you're a horrible singer, you don't have to worry. They have to give it to you."

He looked around for a second too, but then his eyes returned to me, and he shook his head. "No, I mean help me get Regan to like me."

I stared at him while my face got even more prickly. "What? You can't do that. You can't like Regan."

He frowned. "Why not?"

Yeah, Bea, why? "Because she's going to be Annie."

"What does that have to do with anything?"

"Annie becomes Daddy Warbucks's daughter! You can't date *your daughter*!"

Jeremy barked out a laugh. "Bea, it's just a play. It's not real. She won't really be my daughter!"

"But...but..." But nothing. My brain had stopped working.

That's when Carly, who I hadn't even realized had been standing so close to us, took the opportunity to jump in. "Bea's just upset you like Regan because *she* has this HUGE crush on you. Why do you think she tried to kiss you earlier?"

I stood there and stared at the wicked, hateful girl who had just RUINED MY LIFE.

"Shut up," I squeaked.

She snorted. "Great comeback, Spotty."

"Is that true, Bea?" Jeremy asked, making it SO. MUCH. WORSE. "I mean, I didn't really think you were trying to kiss me, but…"

In science class we had learned about this thing called the fight-or-flight response. When animals feel threatened, they either stand their ground and fight back, or they take off to save themselves.

As I bolted out of there, I'd never wished harder for a real pair of wings.

THIRTEEN

My cabinmates were all at the evening program in the mess hall. If I wasn't at the auditions, I was supposed to be there with them, but I couldn't do it. I had just been SO HUMILIATED that all I could do was run to the cabin, climb up onto my bunk and be by myself, away from anyone.

Which is exactly what I did.

It was official. I could never, ever talk to Jeremy again. Thanks to Carly, meanest mean girl on all of Planet Earth, he now knew I had a crush on him. Dad was wrong—not every situation had a silver lining. There was no silver lining here. I just had to figure out a way to never be near Jeremy again.

At least there was no chance of my being in the play now, since I'd run out on the auditions.

And Regan.

The girl Jeremy *really* liked.

Camp Shalom was already a disaster. And I still had four weeks minus two days left here. How had everything gone so wrong in just two days?

Thinking about it made me cry even harder. So hard that I started to hiccup and couldn't stop. And *that* made me cry harder still, because the hiccups hurt and made me feel like a baby. I buried myself under all the covers and wailed away like a deranged coyote.

"Bea? Why aren't you at tryouts?"

Ugh! Can't I just be alone?

I made a ginormous effort to stop crying, but my body wasn't done. I sniffled and hiccupped before I could squeak out, "Please leave me alone!"

"Bea," Julie said from right beside my bunk. "Come on. Tell me what's wrong."

"No," I said from under the covers, where I was practically suffocating. Not that I cared.

Julie put her hand on my back and rubbed in light circles. I could feel it even through the blankets. It made me cry again because it was something my mom would have done. And I wished she were my mom. Not that I was a baby who missed her mommy or anything. It's just that in your worst times, moms hug you and know just what to say to make you feel like you're not alone. Even though they've seen you do silly things and get embarrassed, it's nothing horrible like your *crush* seeing it.

Of course, there was no way I was going to tell Mom about the non-kiss or anything. That fact definitely was NOT going to make it into a letter home.

Then suddenly I *did* care that I was suffocating, because I really couldn't breathe, so I pulled back the covers just enough to let in some fresh air.

"Bea," Julie said a third time, sounding a bit stern.

"What?"

"You need to tell me what's wrong."

"Fine." I threw back the covers completely and sat up, taking a deep breath before I went on. "I was walking back from the bathhouse, and those meanies pushed me into a boy and said I'd tried to kiss him. Then tonight at auditions, they told him I have a crush on him." I paused while Julie stared at me, waiting for more. I dropped my eyes and added, "Maybe it's true abut the crush, so I have been UTTERLY humiliated and can NEVER show my face outside this cabin ever again! Okay? Now you know."

"And it looks like the hives are back."

Fresh tears fell from my eyes. "Right, of course. The hives are back."

"Wait." Julie frowned, her brow wrinkling up. "What meanies? Who pushed you?"

I opened my mouth and then shut it again. If I told on Carly and Samantha, they'd hate me even more.

"I don't know," I said, which was kind of true since I actually hadn't seen which one had done it.

Julie cocked her head to the side. "What do you mean, you don't know?"

"They did it from behind."

"Was it Carly?"

I shrugged but kind of nodded at the same time. "Her or Samantha." But even if it *was* Samantha who'd done the actual pushing, Carly had to be behind it. Everyone knew she was the evil mastermind of the Tiara Twins.

"But please don't get them in trouble, Julie— they hate me already."

"They don't hate you."

Are you serious? "They totally humiliated me. In front of a boy. On purpose. What do you call that?"

Julie sighed. "I'm going to have to talk to the camp directors."

"Oh great. Then they'll get in trouble and hate me more."

Julie pursed her lips. "You might be right. I don't want to make things more uncomfortable for you. How about I talk to them and give them a warning? If they pull another stunt like that, I'm going to the directors."

They'd still hate me. "Couldn't you just not do anything?"

She shook her head. "No. We don't tolerate bullying, and their getting physical with you can't be ignored. They can't get away with what they did. You understand that, right?"

"I guess," I said, wiping at my face with the corner of my sleeve.

"Come on down from there, and let's get you cleaned up. It's almost time for evening snack. You don't want to miss that, do you?"

I rolled my eyes. "Right. I'm having the most devastating day EVER, and a cookie will make it all better. Um, no. I'm not a toddler."

Julie smiled. "You're funny. Okay, we'll nix the snack, but let's dry those tears, shall we?"

I climbed down and followed her to the bathroom, where I pulled some toilet paper off the roll to dab at my eyes, which were now burning too. Like it wasn't enough that my face felt pricklier than ever? As I turned back toward her, she was looking at me strangely.

"Hmmm," she said, tilting her head.

"What?" I asked.

"The hives seem worse."

I tossed the paper into the trash and looked in the mirror.

Gah! She was right. The hives were WAY worse, and it wasn't just because my face was blotchy from crying—there were even more bumps than before, and they were bigger now. Great.

Was I destined to spend the entire summer with hideous spots? Would I forever be known as Spotty?

Julie crossed her arms. "Did you use the cream?"

"Not since this morning."

"Where is it? Let's try it, and if that doesn't work to settle them down, it's back to the infirmary."

That seemed reasonable. I went and got the tube, and Julie helped me smear the white goop all over my face.

"I don't want to go out right now," I said quietly as she replaced the cap on the cream.

Julie nodded. "Okay. Why don't you just lie down for a bit before the rest of the girls come back? You've had a tough day."

I *was* pretty tired—I even yawned just then. I also liked the idea of being in bed when everyone got back, so they couldn't see me. Because not only did I not want them to see me, but I also wasn't ready to face Regan yet.

"Bea?"

Someone was shaking me. Violently.

I bolted upright. "What? Is there a fire?"

"Shhhhh!" Regan said, clamping a hand over my mouth.

It took a second to calm my thumping heart. Okay, so no fire. "What's going on?" I tried to say, but her hand made it come out all muffled.

"I need to talk to you," she whispered. "Come to the bathroom."

About the last thing I wanted to do was get out of my warm bed, but now that Regan had woken me up, I had to pee anyway. So with a groan, I got out of bed and climbed down, sliding my feet into my slippers, waiting for me on the cold wooden floor. Judging by the quietness of the cabin— only the sounds of deep breathing cut through the nighttime silence—I figured it had to be late. Really late.

I didn't remember everyone coming back to the cabin. I must have fallen into a deep sleep.

Regan and I padded quietly toward the bathroom, but when we were halfway there, someone muttered something and moved in their bunk, making us freeze in our tracks.

Then we heard the unmistakable squeak of a fart. We looked at each other, and even in the dark, I could see a glint in Regan's eye as we both tried not to laugh. We hurried the rest of the way to the bathroom.

Without even turning on the light, Regan silently closed and locked the door behind us, and then we both let out our laughter, still trying to be as quiet as possible. "Who was that?" I asked.

"I don't know. One of the Tiara Twins, I reckon."

"Probably."

Then there was silence. Awkward silence, because I was thinking about Jeremy liking her and she was thinking about...well, I didn't know what she was thinking about, but I couldn't get Jeremy out of my head.

"So," she finally said, "I got the part."

I'm a horrible friend! I didn't even ask her about the audition! "Of course you did!" I said, throwing my arms around her and kind of bashing her in the face because it was really dark in the bathroom. There was just a tiny bit of moonlight coming in through the window. "Congratulations!"

"Thanks, Bea. But what about you? Why did you run off?"

Right. "Didn't the girls tell you what happened?"

"What girls?"

"The Tiara Twins?"

"No. I didn't talk to them."

I took a breath and then just blurted it out. "Carly told Jeremy I have a crush on him."

She stared at me for a second, and then her eyes narrowed. "Oh, that horrible, wicked girl."

"It gets worse."

Regan didn't say anything, so I had to tell her, even though I didn't want to.

"Jeremy has a crush on someone. But it's not me."

"Oh, Bea," she said sadly.

"Don't you get it, Regan?" I squeaked. "It's *you*."

There was a very long pause before she said, "But…maybe he likes both of us."

Obviously she was just trying to be nice. And I did appreciate that. But I knew the truth. "No. He told me himself. He asked me to get you to like him."

"He didn't."

"He did."

She sighed.

"You don't like him, do you?" I asked. *Please, please, PLEASE don't like him.* I thought really hard as I held my breath, making a desperate wish that she would say the right thing.

"Well, he's rather sweet and handsome and sings nicely, but it wouldn't be right for me to go out with him, now would it?"

I exhaled in relief. "So you *don't* like him?"

"Even if I did, it wouldn't matter."

Suddenly there was a knock at the door, making me jump. "Hurry up in there!" someone said. "I have to pee, and you've been in there forever!"

"One minute," Regan said to whoever was out there. "We'd better go," she whispered to me.

"You go," I said. "I need to pee. I'll be out in a second."

Regan slipped out, and I turned on the light and locked the door behind her. I heard her talking quietly to the girl outside the door. As I turned toward the toilet, I realized that Regan had never actually said she didn't like Jeremy.

FOURTEEN

We got into a routine at camp—get up, do whatever activity was on the agenda, have lunch, do more activities. During free time and after dinner, Regan went to *Annie* rehearsals, leaving me to work on my friendship bracelet or write letters home.

Regan bugged me to come with her to rehearsals at first, but there was no way I could face Jeremy. And anyway, it turned out they didn't need help with sets or anything because they had premade ones from years before. So there weren't any back-stage jobs.

Just as well, right?

"Okay, girls!" Penny hollered from the back of the cabin one morning. "Up and at 'em!"

The morning chorus of groans began as soon as the lights came on, even though it was already pretty bright in the cabin. I had been awake for a while but didn't want to get out of bed, so I just lay there, running through *Annie* in my head.

Regan had already left the cabin—she liked to get up early and go out into the woods. The counselors didn't mind as long as she didn't go far and stayed on the trails to avoid poison ivy. I thought she was ridiculous for leaving her warm bed before she had to, but she said she liked to be outside. Maybe she was out there practicing for the play, and if that was the case, I was glad she hadn't asked me to come with her. Not that I wasn't happy for Regan, being in the play. I just didn't want to hear about practices and what Jeremy did.

Well, sometimes I *did* want to hear about Jeremy, and I'd ask her about rehearsal during our evening snack time. Then she'd start telling me, and I'd be sorry for asking. I couldn't help myself.

On this morning, as I waited for the rest of the girls to use the bathroom, Carly came up to my bunk and just stood there, smirking.

"What?" I asked.

"Where's your friend?"

"I don't know."

"Maybe she's gone to meet your boyfriend. Or should I say *her* boyfriend."

I pushed myself against the bunk, so I was sitting up. I didn't want to even talk to Carly, but I had to defend Regan. "Jeremy isn't her boyfriend. Just because he likes her that doesn't mean anything."

"Oh, right. So it doesn't mean anything that she was *kissing* your boyfriend last night?"

"He's not my boyfri—wait. What?" My heart stopped as my brain caught up with what she'd said.

Carly crossed her arms, looking even more smug, if that was possible. Which apparently it was.

"You heard me. Your new BFF and your Jeremy were kissing last night after rehearsal. I saw them behind the lodge."

She'd seen them kissing? Could she be telling the truth? Was it possible Regan had kissed Jeremy and then decided to keep it from me? No. It *wasn't* possible. She'd had plenty of opportunity to tell me and apologize. And, of course, she would have felt UTTER and COMPLETE shame and would have BEGGED for my forgiveness, which I would have granted, after some tears and promises from her that she would never, ever speak with Jeremy again. You know, other than what was absolutely necessary for the production.

That's what would have happened if Carly was telling me the truth.

"You're lying. You're just mad because Regan got the part of Annie and Samantha didn't."

She shrugged. "What do I care? And anyway, I'm telling the truth." She nodded her head toward the other side of the cabin. "Ask Emily. She was with me."

I glanced over at Emily, who would have been at the rehearsal, as she was in the play too. She nodded. "I saw them. That's sure what it looked like anyway." Emily wasn't really friends with Carly and Samantha, so she had no reason to lie. At least she didn't look smug about it—she even seemed sorry.

My heart sank. I actually felt it drop into my stomach and roll around.

Carly laughed. "Told you! Why don't you ask your little foreign friend what she knows about *French kissing?*"

"She's Irish," I said.

Carly rolled her eyes. "Whatev."

"Why are you doing this?" I asked.

She cocked her head at me and gave a little shrug. "I'm not doing anything. I'm not the one who kissed him. I just thought you'd want to know what your friend is up to while you're stuck in the cabin with spots all over you. Nice face, by the way."

I tried to think of a witty reply, but nothing came to mind. All I could think was, Regan. Kissed. Jeremy. My ONE friend at camp had betrayed me in the worst way possible.

By the time I got dressed, the bathroom was free, so I used it and then went out to the sinks to wash my hands. I was on total autopilot, unable to pay attention to anything because all I could think about was the horror of Regan kissing Jeremy.

Regan KISSING Jeremy.

Regan kissing JEREMY.

REGAN KISSING JEREMY!

It was DEVASTATING. How could she do that when she knew how much I liked him? How did it happen? And why didn't she tell me? She should have come clean. Yes, I would have been mad, but telling me was the right thing to do. I thought she was my friend. My good friend, and the kind of person who wouldn't steal my guy. Even if he wasn't *officially* my guy, but just the guy I *wanted* to be my guy.

What was I supposed to do now?

With a big sigh, I turned off the tap and looked into the mirror as I scratched at an itchy spot on my—

Oh.

My.

Face.

"So let's see...they were getting better, but then they got worse, and now they are—"

"The worst they've ever been," I interrupted. "LOOK AT ME!"

But I didn't need to say that because Lisa *was* looking at me. She hadn't stopped looking at me since Julie and I had arrived at the infirmary first thing. I had even skipped breakfast. I didn't need the entire camp seeing what I looked like. Because I looked awful.

"What did you eat?"

"Nothing. Not even a snack or breakfast."

"Any more traipsing in the woods?"

"No."

"Well," she said, rolling her stool over and looking at my face very closely, "it's definitely a reaction of some sort. I'd like to give you a shot of something a little stronger this time. Are you okay with a needle?"

I took a deep breath and nodded.

She got off her stool and went to her medicine cabinet to get out her supplies. "So…" she said over her shoulder.

"So what?"

"I would like to get to the bottom of what's causing these hives. It doesn't appear to be food or some sort of environmental allergen." She turned back to me, holding a little vial and a plastic wrapper that she opened to reveal a syringe. She took it out and filled it with liquid from the vial.

I shrugged. "I don't know. They seem to pop up at the weirdest times. Like when I least want them."

Lisa froze for a second and looked at me, only this time she wasn't looking at my spots, but right into my eyes.

It made me feel weird and fidgety. "What?"

She glanced down at the syringe and then shook her head and came at me with the needle, not saying anything. I hoped she wasn't going to put it in my butt. The thought of that made me feel a bit dizzy, but I steeled myself—even if I had to take the shot in the butt, it was better than the hives. Especially since they'd started to get really itchy.

"Roll up your sleeve," she said, nodding toward my arm.

Relieved, I pulled up my sleeve and held it out of the way. She wiped a patch of my skin with a cold alcohol pad before she pinched the flesh of my arm a bit. She counted down from three and then I felt a sting for a few seconds. Then it was over. I was pretty proud of myself for not freaking out. Stevie'd had a meltdown the last time Mom took him for a shot. I'd heard him screaming from where I sat in the waiting room, which had made me think they were doing a lot more than giving him a needle, but Mom confirmed later that it was just the shot.

"There you go," Lisa said, giving me a little pat on the shoulder before she put the needle into a yellow box on the counter. Then, before I even knew what to do next, she turned back, looked me right in the eye again and said, "So, Bea, tell me, are you under any stress?"

Am I under any stress? Are you kidding? Let's see. I leave home for the first time, without my best friend, and come to a camp where I know exactly no one. I get bullied by girls who are HEINOUSLY mean, who expose my crush TO my crush, and then I find out the ONE person I thought might be a friend goes and KISSES him. Would YOU be under any stress?

I took a deep, staggered breath in and said what I hoped sounded like a confident "No."

"Bea?"

I looked at the wall. And the canisters of tongue depressors and cotton balls. And the box of gloves on the table. Then at my own hands and my shoes and the floor. Anywhere but at Lisa.

"Bea?" she said more sternly this time, making me look at her. "Are you sure you're not stressed out at all? Stress can manifest in many ways. Nightmares or trouble sleeping, tummy aches, headaches, skin rashes or breakouts, or—"

"Hives," I said.

She nodded. "Hives."

I sighed. "Okay, yes. Maybe I'm a little stressed."

"Want to talk about it?"

"No." *Why do you think I lied in the first place? Duh.*

"You might find it helps."

"When Kylie at school was stressed out because her parents got divorced, they took her to a shrink. I don't think it helped. She was still freaking out after and was actually even more upset because she'd had to quit band so she could go to a shrink."

Lisa nodded. "But sometimes it can really help to talk to someone."

"What do shrinks do exactly?"

"They listen to people talk about what's worrying them so they can help them work out their troubles or stresses."

"That's it? All they do is *talk*?" I asked. I'd been sure it was more than that.

"Mostly," she said. "A lot of people find just talking things out helps. They learn about themselves and why they feel the things they do. Some people also feel comfortable talking to their rabbi or someone else whose job it is to be a good listener." She made it seem like it was no big deal.

But it was a very big deal. And anyway, I just had a lot of bad stuff happening to me. Telling someone about it wasn't going to make all that stuff go away. "I don't think I want to do that." I sure didn't want to tell her or a doctor about my crush and how Regan had betrayed me. I *definitely* didn't want to tell a rabbi that either. Yikes.

"Are you a bit homesick, Bea? It's normal to be afraid and lonely your first time away from your family."

I shrugged. "Maybe. But it's not just that."

She sat down on her stool and rolled toward me again. "You can tell me. I won't say anything to anyone. I just want to help."

I looked at her and almost told her. She was smiling like Mom would have, and I could tell she was being honest when she said she wanted to help. But I couldn't. I just couldn't tell her what the horrible girls had done and how humiliated I'd been. And I couldn't tell her about Regan.

Anyway, it seemed silly now that I'd even felt so close to Regan when I'd only known her for a few days. We weren't like me and Frankie had been. Until Frankie ditched me to go to horse camp.

Why do all my friends betray me?

What is wrong with me?

I'm so alone.

And then, before I knew it, tears were leaking out of me. And no matter how hard I tried, they wouldn't stop. I dropped my head, making the tears fall and splash on my legs.

"Oh, Bea," Lisa said, handing me a tissue.

"I'm sorry," I said. It didn't come out right, but she must have understood.

"You don't need to be sorry. It's okay. It's hard to be away from home. And the hives, well, those aren't helping, are they?"

I shook my head and dabbed at my eyes with the tissue. "I just…they're just…I don't…"

"Shhhh," she said, rubbing the arm that she

hadn't put the shot in. And then she took my hand and squeezed it. "You don't have to talk about it right now if you don't want to."

"I'm just…I'm tired."

And I was. I wanted to crawl back into bed and wake up on Labor Day.

"It's the shot. Come on—you can lie down for a bit." She held my hand as I hopped down from the exam table, ripping off the paper with my butt again and not even caring. I let her lead me down the hall to a bedroom and I sat down on the bed and even let her untie and take off my sneakers. It was a babyish thing to do, but it felt nice to have her taking care of me the way Mom would have if I was sick at home.

"Just lie down, and I'll be back in a little bit, okay?"

I nodded and slid under the blanket, still wearing my clothes. Lisa sat on the edge of the bed and pulled the blanket up and tucked me in like it wasn't weird that I was going back to bed before I'd even eaten any breakfast.

After a few minutes, as I was dozing off, I felt her get up. She left the room, turning out the light and quietly closing the door behind her.

FIFTEEN

I opened my eyes and almost screamed. No, not almost. I *did* scream. Because there was someone standing by the bed, staring at me. I blinked. What I was seeing wasn't really making sense. I figured I must be dreaming. But why would I dream about a tiny alien wearing a New York Yankees baseball cap and a Camp Shalom T-shirt?

"Sorry. I didn't mean to scare you." The words were spoken in a very high voice.

"Who are you?" I asked and then held my breath as I waited for the answer. Maybe the clothes were a disguise. Maybe I was about to be abducted.

I had to be still dreaming. My brain felt so fuzzy. None of this made sense.

"I'm Harry."

"Like, Harry Potter?"

Harry shook his head. "More like Harry Houdini, the most amazing escape artist there ever was. My dad's a big fan. I even have a bunch of movies about him on my iPad."

His dad? I rubbed my eyes until they burned. "Why are you here? And what time is it?"

"I hang out at the infirmary a lot. We met when you were here before, remember? I was stocking the supply closet."

As the fuzz cleared from my brain, a memory surfaced of a kid standing on a stepstool, putting away medical supplies. He seemed so much smaller now. But also very human. *Of course he was human. What was wrong with me?*

"Oh, right. Hi," I said.

"Lisa asked me to come wake you up for lunch."

Lunch? My stomach gurgled, clearly liking the sound of that.

"Excuse me," I muttered, pressing my hand against my empty gut to try to get it to shut up.

Harry laughed. "Just in time, huh? There's sandwiches and salad. Can I bring you a plate?"

I was remembering the first time I'd seen Harry, by the out-of-bounds cottages. I had thought he was pretty young. But listening to the way he talked and joked, now and that time before in the hall, he didn't sound young at all. How old was he really? I looked at him curiously.

"Beatrice?" he said, making me realize I hadn't answered him, that I'd just been staring rudely at him.

I shook my head. "Sorry, still asleep. Please call me Bea," I said. He must have read my name off a chart or something. Grown-ups always put down my full name, no matter what I *wanted* to be called.

"Lisa said you might be drowsy from the shot."

I yawned but covered my mouth so he wouldn't think I had *no* manners. "Yeah, I think I am. I'd love whatever you want to bring. Thanks."

The top of his head was covered by his baseball cap, but when he turned around, I could see that the back was bald. Like, completely bald.

I pushed myself up into a sitting position and leaned against the wall, stretching to try to break out of the drowsy feeling. A few minutes later Harry returned with a paper plate piled high with food in one hand and a bottle of water in the other.

I smiled. "That looks great. Thanks."

He handed me the plate and slid the bottle onto the nightstand beside me. "You're welcome." Then he reached into his back pocket and pulled out a rolled-up napkin and handed it to me. "Silverware," he said as I took it from him. "This is a classy establishment."

That's when I realized that Harry not only was bald, but also didn't have any eyebrows. And as I looked even more closely, I realized he didn't even have any eyelashes either.

"What?" he said, his smile suddenly gone.

How rude ARE you, Bea? Stop staring! "Sorry," I mumbled. "Nothing. I mean, thanks again for the food, Harry."

I figured he must have some kind of cancer. Because cancer makes people lose their hair. Well, cancer treatments do. One of Mom's friends had ovarian cancer. She lost all her hair after chemo. She went into remission and her hair grew back eventually, but before it did, she wore lots of funky head scarves. I thought they looked really nice, but Mom said she was just happy to get her hair back.

"Is it okay if I eat with you?" Harry asked. "It's super busy out there, and I should stay out of the way."

"Of course." I mean, I couldn't say no since he'd just brought me lunch.

He smiled and then ran out to get his food. I waited (not so patiently) because Mom says you can't start eating until everyone is at the table. Or, in this case, the bed. But I didn't have to wait long. Harry was back in just a couple of minutes, a lot less food on his plate than he'd brought for me. He sat on the chair in the corner, carefully unrolled his napkin and took out the cutlery before he laid the cloth on his lap. I noticed his feet didn't reach the floor.

As I went for my fork, Harry started reciting the hamotzi. Yikes! I covered up my move by scratching my ear and quickly joined him in the blessing over the food. Once we were finished, I dug in.

"Thanks again for this," I said between bites.

"It's okay. It's nice to have someone to eat with."

"Don't you eat at the mess hall?" I asked.

He shook his head as he picked up his half sandwich. "I'm not a regular camper, in case you hadn't noticed."

I looked down at my plate, feeling my face heat up. Of course I'd noticed. And I for sure would have seen him at the lodge or in the mess hall before now. At least, *I thought* I would have—in my short time at camp, I'd sort of had a lot on my mind. "Sorry."

"That's not what I meant. Sorry, Beatr—Bea. I didn't mean to make you feel bad. I just hang out here in the infirmary most of the time. I live here. My grandparents started Camp Shalom, and my parents are the camp directors. So I don't have to pay or anything. Not that I do much camp stuff anyway."

I felt bad that he was missing out on all the fun. I wondered how sick he was. He didn't *look* sick. "Don't you do *any* of the activities?" I asked.

Harry took a bite of his sandwich and shrugged, chewing before he replied. "I can if I want. But sometimes the other kids…" His voice trailed off, and he sighed.

I swallowed. "They can be mean."

He looked at me, right into my eyes, and it was obvious I'd been right on. "Yeah. I mean, no one really says anything, but they stare at me and treat me different. Like I'm contagious."

I was going to ask that, but, thankfully, before I could even open my mouth, he added, "I'm not, you know."

"I know!" I said, as though it had NEVER even occurred to me.

"But they act like I am, and it's just easier to avoid them."

And they probably say lots of mean things behind your back too. I bet the Tiara Twins *would be royally, heinously horrible to you.* "Yeah. But isn't it boring being stuck in here all the time?"

"Sometimes, but mostly not. I like it here, learning medical stuff. *And* I get to stock the cupboards!" He said it like it was a *very* exciting job.

I laughed. "Do you want to be a doctor or something when you grow up?"

He stared at me for what seemed like a really long time and then looked down at his plate. "Maybe."

"Well, that's cool then. It's like you're learning on the job."

"Lisa lets me help out with the medical stuff. And sometimes I get to serve nice people lunch."

I smiled at being called nice. We concentrated on eating our lunches for a bit. I was curious about his illness, but I didn't really know him, so it felt wrong to just start asking him all sorts of personal questions. I didn't know a lot about cancer, only that it was a really bad disease that was definitely VERY SERIOUS. Obviously, Harry couldn't have any sort of lady-part cancer like my mom's friend had, but it's rude to ask someone you hardly know about their disease so I didn't ask anything.

I hoped he would talk about it. He didn't. Instead he asked me how I liked my cabin.

I shrugged. "The cabin is fine, but I could do with some new people in it."

"What do you mean?"

I told him about Carly and Samantha being so mean to me and about Regan betraying me, but I left out the Jeremy details. I couldn't tell a person I had just met—especially a boy—about my crush. WAY too embarrassing!

"That stinks," Harry said, wiping his mouth with his napkin. I liked that he had such nice manners.

"Yeah. And now I can't help out with *Annie*."

"You mean the play? Why not?"

Wasn't it obvious? "Because they're all in it, and I can't face Jere—Regan or any of them again."

"But they're in your cabin. You'll have to see them soon."

"I guess. But I don't have to talk to them. If I was helping with the play, I'd have to talk to them all the time." *And see Jeremy and Regan together. And maybe stumble on them kissing behind the lodge. No, thank you.*

I shrugged and ate the last bite of my sandwich.

"It's not a big deal. It was just something to do, I guess," I said. Which, of course, was a huge lie. But I hoped Harry didn't pick up on it. "It just stinks not having any friends here."

"I don't have any friends here either," Harry said, his eyes down on his plate.

My heart hurt when he said it. I hated that kids really could be so mean. But not *all* of them were.

"Well, you do now," I said. "We both do, right?"

Harry looked up, and it seemed to take a second for him to realize I meant me. "Thanks, Bea. Yeah," he said with a big grin.

I smiled back. Dad would be proud that I'd found a silver lining after all.

A little while later Harry and I were watching YouTube clips of *Annie* on his iPad, because he'd never seen it. I wanted to ask him how old he was but didn't want to hurt his feelings. Maybe the cancer made it so he didn't grow very well. I mean, he was smaller than my little brother, but he spoke like he was older than him and was WAY more mature. And he was obviously really smart too. But I didn't want to be rude, so I kept my mouth shut and concentrated on the videos.

As we watched, my heart wanted me to sing along with the songs, but I couldn't do that in front of Harry. I just sort of hummed along quietly. Lisa came in about halfway through "It's the Hard-Knock Life."

"I see my assistant has fed and entertained you," she said with a smile, tapping a finger on the brim of Harry's cap.

He grinned at her, adjusting his cap. "Well, I fed her, but she's entertaining me, showing me *Annie*. Or at least parts of it."

"Maybe you can watch the whole thing on Netflix," I suggested.

Lisa scanned my face. "How're you feeling, Bea?"

"Better, thanks."

She nodded and then glanced over at Harry. "I need to give Bea the once-over. Thanks again for helping out, Harry."

Harry took that as his cue to leave and scooched off his chair. "It was nice to meet you, Bea. Thanks for showing me *Annie*."

"Thanks for bringing me lunch. It was fun hanging out with you," I said.

He smiled and then turned and left, closing the door behind him.

"I hope you don't mind that I sent in my helper. I got swamped out there, but I wanted to make sure you got some lunch," said Lisa.

"It's okay. He's really nice."

She smiled as she sat down on the edge of the bed. "He's had a pretty tough go, but yeah, he is a great kid. Thanks."

I shrugged. "You don't have to thank me. I like him."

She frowned and looked away. "It's just…well, like I said, he's had it rough, and he doesn't spend a lot of time with kids his age."

"How old is he?" I asked.

"Thirteen. He had his bar mitzvah a few months ago."

Thirteen? Older than me! It was hard to believe we were so close in age.

"The hives look better. How does your face feel?"

"Still a bit prickly and itchy, but definitely better. I'm still kind of tired though." Which was true. But I also wasn't eager to go back to the cabin. What would I say to Regan? And the second I left the infirmary, I'd have to rejoin my cabin in whatever activity was on this afternoon's agenda. I yawned and made my eyes droopy. "Can I stay here a bit longer?"

She frowned and looked at me sideways. I knew that look—Mom gave me the same one when I said I had a stomach ache right before Sunday Hebrew school. Lisa wasn't buying it.

I tried a different strategy. "Maybe I could hang out with Harry some more. He seemed to really enjoy my company. And maybe we could watch *Annie* together. I think he'd really like that."

She lifted her eyebrows, and I thought I was going to get sent packing, but she sighed. "Fine. One night here. But you're going back to your cabin first thing in the morning. Deal?"

"Deal." That gave me a whole afternoon and night to figure out what to do about the Regan situation.

SIXTEEN

Even though I'd had lots of time to figure out what to say to Regan, I still hadn't. Maybe because I really didn't want to deal with it, or maybe because I was absolutely stumped. Part of it, though, was that Harry had come back and we'd played games on his iPad all afternoon.

"I wish you could stay here all the time," he said at five o'clock. Lisa had just popped her head in and reminded him he had to meet his parents and that it was just about time for my dinner anyway. The good news was, I didn't have to go to the mess hall to get it. Julie was coming to visit and would bring it to me.

"Me too," I said to Harry. And I really meant it. He was fun to hang out with, and I didn't have to worry about the mean Tiara Twins, confronting Regan or seeing Jeremy. "But I don't think Lisa will let me stay. My hives are clearing up."

"Your face looks a lot better," he said.

"Thanks."

"Although it's not like I care what you look like. Looks aren't as important as what's on the inside. You could have spots like a Dalmatian, and I wouldn't care."

At first I smiled, but then I looked away as I really thought about what he'd said. It made me feel guilty.

"What?" he asked. "What did I say?"

I shook my head. "It's not that. I…I feel really bad about something."

"What do you mean?"

"I…well, when I first saw you before…"

"You didn't like how I looked?" he asked in a soft voice. It broke my heart a little.

"No, it's not that I didn't like how you looked. Er…I uh…" I suddenly felt really stupid. I couldn't tell him what I'd thought when I'd first woken up!

"What is it?" he said.

"No, never mind."

"Whatever it is, I've heard worse," he said. Which was supposed to make me feel better but didn't—it made me feel *more* horrible.

"I can't…"

"Bea…"

I exhaled. "Fine. I thought you were an alien. I mean, I woke up all groggy after the shot and you were standing there and you kind of scared me! I'm really, really sorry, Harry." I tensed up, waiting for him to yell or maybe even cry.

He barked out a laugh. Which was NOT AT ALL what I had expected.

"You think that's funny?"

"Yeah. You thought I was an *alien*? Like, from outer space?"

I nodded. "I don't see how that's funny. But I wasn't trying to be mean or anything."

"I know you weren't trying to be mean, Bea. I did wake you up, and you weren't expecting me there, so I get it." He snorted. "You think I don't know what I look like? That I'm different? I've heard a lot worse things. People stare and point all the time. So it's not a big deal that you thought that. And really, I don't think you were trying to be mean," he said again.

"I wasn't, I swear!" I said. And then, after a moment, added, "So you're not mad?"

"No, Queen Bea, I'm not mad."

I looked at him, surprised. "Only my dad calls me Queen Bea. Wait," I said, "did you already know that because you ARE an alien and you've been watching my house through satellite surveillance or whatever it is you aliens use to spy on us humans?" We were both laughing now.

"Yes. Meep, meep," he said in a robot voice while

doing a jerky dance with his arms. "Take me to your leader."

"You're funny, Harry."

"HARRY!" Lisa called from down the hall. "Now!"

"I'd better go. My alien superiors…er, *my parents* will be waiting for me," he said with a very obvious wink.

I grinned at him. "Thanks for hanging out with me today."

"I had fun too."

And then, before it got weird and awkward because I had no idea when I'd see him again, even though I really wanted to, he left.

Eight minutes later, Julie arrived.

But she wasn't alone.

"Hi, Bea," Julie said as she came into the room with a big tinfoil-wrapped package, Regan trailing behind her. "We brought you pizza. We didn't know what kind you liked, so we brought two slices each of veggie pepperoni with mushroom, and plain cheese."

"Thanks, *Julie*," I said. I did appreciate the pizza, especially because it smelled amazing, but I was trying to pretend Regan wasn't even there. It worked for about three seconds.

"Hi, Bea," Regan said with a big smile. She didn't look sorry or regretful AT ALL, which made me think Carly hadn't told her that she'd blabbed about her and Jeremy. She didn't look guilty, either, making me think she was *quite* the actress. *Good thing she's the lead in the play.*

"What are *you* doing here?" I asked, looking at her but not meeting her eyes.

Her face fell. "I wanted to visit you and make sure you were okay." *Because that's what friends do*, I'm sure she was thinking.

Except friends don't kiss friends' boyfriends. Or, in my case, boys that friends *want* to be boyfriends.

"I'm fine," I said, which was a huge, fat lie.

"Everything okay, Bea?" Julie asked, obviously picking up on my frosty attitude.

"Just fine," I repeated.

"How come you have to stay here?" Regan asked. "You look a lot better."

I picked an imaginary piece of lint off my shirt and flicked it away, totally avoiding looking at her. "They gave me a shot, and it knocked me out, and I need quiet and rest," I said. Which was mostly true.

I yawned, not bothering to cover my open mouth. "But I'm really tired now, so I think I should just eat and go back to sleep. Thanks for bringing the pizza. *Julie.*"

"See you tomorrow," Regan said, sounding a little unsure.

"Yeah. Bye," I said rudely. I *knew* it was rude, and I sort of cringed on the inside, but I couldn't help it. She'd kissed Jeremy! What was I supposed to be like, all *let's be BFFs?*

Not likely.

They *finally* left, leaving me to eat my pizza.

Alone.

I really wished Harry could have stayed. I was tired, like I'd told Julie and Regan, but not *that* tired, and it would have been nice to hang out with Harry and watch *Annie* or play more games.

"Bea?" Lisa said from the doorway. Another woman wearing scrubs stood beside her.

"Yeah?"

"I'm leaving for the day. This is Claudia. She's here for the night shift. Let her know if you need anything, okay?"

"Hi, Bea," Claudia said with a smile.

"Oh." For some reason I'd thought Lisa lived at the infirmary and would be there the whole time. Obviously not. "Hi," I said to Claudia.

"Now don't give her any trouble," Lisa said with a wink.

I rolled my eyes. "Please."

"See you tomorrow, Bea. But don't forget—you're out of here in time to meet your cabin at breakfast."

I nodded. "Got it. Thanks."

And then *they* were gone, and I was all alone again. There weren't any TVs in the infirmary, and there was no other technology for miles around—Harry had his iPad, but he wasn't here. Dad had assured me I wouldn't miss my phone because I'd be too busy having fun, but guess what? I *totally* missed my phone.

Not that I had anyone to text. Frankie didn't have her phone either, and, well, there was no one else. But I was SO bored!

With a sigh, I got up to pee and then asked Claudia for a pen and paper so I could write a letter home.

SEVENTEEN

Julie came to pick me up well before breakfast, which was a good thing since I didn't have a change of clothes or anything and needed a shower.

The screen door to the infirmary had just slammed closed behind us, when I was instantly sorry she'd picked me up at all. She immediately wanted to know what was going on between me and Regan.

Obviously my attitude the night before had tipped her off. But denial seemed like a good course of action. "Nothing."

"Bea," she said, sounding like my mom.

"It's between us."

Julie wasn't giving up. "Regan was very upset last night after we left you."

I shrugged. I was pretty upset too, but that was Regan's fault, not mine.

"I thought you two were getting along great."

"Well, now we're not," I said in what I hoped was an *and that's final* voice.

Nope. "Bea, come on. Tell me what happened. It's usually not as big a deal as you think it is."

Oh, really? A kiss is no big deal? And here I'd thought Julie got it and wasn't just a clueless grown-up. "It's a very big deal," I muttered.

"Is it because she's in *Annie* and you're not? Because I can get you a part in it if you want. You can be an extra orphan or something. There's always room for more—"

I stopped walking and looked up at her. "It's not that, okay? I don't want to talk about it, but Regan and I aren't friends anymore."

Julie took a breath and crossed her arms. "Bea,

it's fine if you don't want to talk to me about it. But you need to talk to Regan. At least tell her what she did wrong."

Right. Like Regan had NO IDEA she kissed Jeremy. Like maybe she tripped and fell right onto his lips or something.

But the more I thought about it, the more something started to bother me. Regan wasn't stupid. If she'd kissed Jeremy, she would have known I'd be upset if I found out. And if what Julie was saying was true, she seemed to have no idea. Could she really have no clue what she had done wrong?

OR...

Maybe Carly had lied. Maybe Regan hadn't actually kissed Jeremy, and the mean girl was just trying to break us up and had somehow gotten Emily to go along with it.

I needed to find out the truth about what had *really* happened.

I didn't get an opportunity to talk to Regan privately until just before lunch. By the time I had gotten to breakfast, there were no seats near her. Right after that we had waterskiing. I'd thought this would give us some time together while we waited for our turns, but she had brought a note to camp saying she had some sort of inner-ear thing and couldn't waterski, so she got to sit in the boat the whole time—which, if you ask me, looked like a lot more fun than trying to waterski. Waterskiing looked scary.

I sat on the dock by myself, ignoring Carly and Samantha (who were pretty much ignoring me—Julie told me they'd gotten in trouble for the pushing incident) and trying not to freak out about waterskiing. I watched the other girls falling on their faces in the water and getting pulled along by the boat when they forgot to let go of the rope. (Note: If you ever try waterskiing and fall down, LET GO OF THE ROPE!)

And then, when it was my turn, I flat out said no. Yup, I completely and totally chickened out. No amount of encouragement from Penny or Julie was going to make me go out there and get pulled along like a floppy dead fish tied to a rope. It didn't look like any kind of fun, and the last thing I needed was to hurt myself AND look stupid in front of all the girls.

Again.

So there I sat in my still-dry bathing suit, wondering why Frankie and I had been so excited about camp in the first place.

After waterskiing (or not waterskiing), we all went back to the cabin to change for lunch. Since Regan was still dry too, we both hung out on opposite ends of the front porch of the cabin, waiting for everyone else. It was weird, because we both knew something was up and that we should talk about it, but neither of us knew how to begin. *I* sure didn't.

Eventually Regan did. "Hey, Bea," she said quietly.

"Hey."

She walked over to me and stood close. She looked over her shoulder before she whispered, "Did I do something wrong, Bea?"

I took a deep breath. "Carly said—"

She frowned and interrupted me. "You listened to *anything* that *horrible girl* said?"

I exhaled in relief. "So it's not true."

"What's not true?"

"You didn't kiss Jeremy?"

She stared at me and blinked several times. AND DIDN'T SAY NO.

"You kissed him."

"It's not what it seems, Bea."

"I thought you were my friend!"

"I *am* your friend," she said, grabbing for my hand.

I ripped it away from her.

"Bea! Let me explain what happened."

"I know what happened. You kissed him. You kissed Jeremy. Carly was right! I can't believe it. I'm so stupid."

"No, Bea. You're not stupid, but you need to understand."

"I understand just fine. You pretended to be my friend just to get close to Jeremy, and then you stole him. I never want to talk to you again."

She opened her mouth to say something, but just then the rest of the girls came out. Conversation over.

Later, at the mess hall, Regan kept trying to catch my attention—I could feel her looking at me from the other side of the table, but I kept my eyes on my plate, making it seem like my salad was VERY INTERESTING.

Which, believe me, it wasn't.

After lunch we had A&C, which reminded me of the half-finished friendship bracelet I had back at the cabin. HA! What a laugh. Like I was going to give that to Regan now.

"Bea, I really need to talk to you." Regan was standing right behind me.

"I told you," I said in a low voice, not wanting to make a BIG SCENE in the A&C cabin. "I never want to speak to you again."

"But—"

I held up my hand. "Did your mouth touch Jeremy's mouth?"

"Well…not exactly…but you need to—"

I cut her off again. "I don't care. You betrayed me. We're not friends anymore. I don't think we ever were. And if you talk to me again, I will scream."

She shut her mouth, turned around and walked away. For some reason that made no sense at all, I felt kind of bad about the whole thing. I mean, I hadn't betrayed HER.

I heard a snicker from the other side of the room. I looked over and there were Carly and

Samantha, sitting at the table with the big scrap-booking kit in front of them.

"Aw, spotty little Bea got stung," Carly said, sticking her bottom lip out.

Even though I had wanted to make some special greeting cards with the scrapbooking supplies, I was in no mood for the Tiara Twins, so I just ignored them and went to find Abby.

"I left my project back at the cabin. Can I go get it?" I asked. Maybe I could just go wander around outside until A&C was over. It wasn't like I was feeling overly creative anyway.

"Isn't there something here you can do?" Abby replied.

"No."

She glanced from me to the rest of the girls and back to me and then said, "How would you like to help me with something?"

I shrugged.

"How are you on the computer?"

"Pretty good, I guess."

"Great. How about helping me design the *Annie* program?"

YES! Something I can do! I nodded, and Abby took me to the back, where her computer was. She showed me the software she was using and let me take it over.

So that was pretty cool.

And the best part? I got to do it on my own, and the time passed super quickly. Before I knew it, Julie was standing over me, telling me it was snack time.

The rest of the day was spent dodging people. The Tiara Twins, Regan and Julie, who I was worried wanted to give me another lecture about talking to Regan.

Dodging people is exhausting. And kind of lonely. Actually, *very* lonely.

The only good thing about that whole day was the letters I'd received, which I got to read after the evening program.

I'd changed into my pajamas after returning to the cabin so I could be up on my bunk before Regan got into her bed (again—exhausting to figure all this stuff out). So while the other girls talked, I sat on my bed and tore the letters open, more excited than I'd thought I would be to read about what was going on at home. Mom and Dad had sent one each, and even Stevie had written one, which was tucked inside Mom's envelope.

And there was one from Frankie. My stomach did a lurch when I saw her messy handwriting on the envelope. Of course she'd have the camp's address, since her brother was here, so I shouldn't have been too surprised, but I was.

I was going to read it last, but then I opened it first, thinking I'd get it over with. I thought about throwing it in the trash, because the *last* thing I needed was to read about her riding and getting to hang out with horses all day, but she was still my best friend, so I couldn't bring myself to do it.

With a deep breath, I unfolded the page.

>*Hi, Bea,*
>
>*I miss you! xoxo. I hope you are having fun at Camp Shalom. I bet you are having fun doing arts and crafts and swimming and everything. Horse camp is SOOOOO MUUUUCH harder than we thought! We have to clean horse poo (disgusting!) and stinky straw and clean and brush the horses all the time, even picking all the junk out of their hooves! It's like we are their personal maids. It's so hard and my arms get tired from having to brush them all the time. Today I was braiding Sunfire's tail and he pooped right as*

I was standing there! Ugh. SO GROSS!
Do you see Jeremy a lot? My mom said
I had to write him a letter and I guess
maybe he'll write me one, but I haven't
gotten one yet. Can you ask him if he's
written me one yet?

There are some girls here who are
nice, but they're not you, so I'm not
going to be best friends with them.
You're a way better friend than ANY of
them. I hope you are not too lonely, but
I hope you don't get a new best friend.
Just kidding! Maybe. Xoxo

Write back! Please! Miss you!
Hugs, your BEST FRIEND,
Frankie Ferstein

I read Frankie's letter three times. At first I was glad
she had to clean up all the poop, like Regan did with

Taffy, but then I just missed her. And that made me sad. I was lonely, and it sounded like she was too. What a horrible summer this was turning out to be.

I took a breath and put her letter back into its envelope, then took out the one from Stevie. It didn't seem like it was going to be all that sincere when it started out with:

> Dear BEATRICE,
> Mom and Dad say I have to write you a
> letter, so here's me writing you a letter.

I'm sure he thought writing out my whole name in caps would make me mad, but it actually made me laugh and even miss him. A little.

I laughed again as I read the rest of it, because I could "hear" his voice, like how in movies you hear the person reading the letter they wrote even though they're not there when the person they sent it to is reading it.

They say I'm supposed to tell you that I hope you're having a good time but you only left this morning so I guess I hope you had a good bus ride. I'm going to have a GREAT summer. I'm going to play lots of video games and go swimming at Jimmy's house. It will be nice to have the bathroom to myself, but I guess I might miss you a little. Have fun at camp. Steven

"Oh, so it's Steven now?" I said out loud. Then I read his letter again, and Mom's and Dad's too. They didn't have much to say, since they'd written the day I left. Dad reminded me to look for silver linings. Mom included a little painting of the tree in our backyard. I felt bad about how I'd insulted her about her art before. She really is a good painter, and I'm not just saying that because she's my mom.

I looked at the painting for a while and then put it on the windowsill behind my bunk so I could look at it whenever I wanted to. I slid all the letters under my pillow.

"Two minutes to lights-out," Shira called out from the back of the cabin.

I got under the covers, even though I wasn't really sleepy. Neither were the other girls, judging by the whispers around me. I didn't care that they were probably whispering about me.

Okay, yes I did. But I *wanted* not to care. I wanted DESPERATELY not to care. I rolled over so I didn't have to see them. And then I heard the squeak under me—Regan was getting into bed.

I slid my hand underneath my pillow so I could feel the letters from home.

EIGHTEEN

When Julie announced we would be playing hide-and-seek and the winner would win a five-dollar credit at the tuckshop to spend on candy, I thought of the perfect hiding place. I'd seen a stand of bushes on the way to the infirmary that I could crawl under. Maybe if I won and shared my prize with some of the other girls, they'd be nicer to me.

But the bushes were a bit far from home base, and when Julie started counting, she counted fast, so I had to sprint to get the spot before anyone else did. Unfortunately the universe had other plans for me, and as I came to an uneven patch of ground, I fell and twisted my ankle. It was VERY painful.

At first I tried to stand, so I could get to the hiding spot, but then I realized my ankle was not at all interested in that plan.

And the silver lining to spraining your ankle at camp? If you whine and cry enough, they'll let you call home. And if you whine and cry enough to your parents about your cabin and all the stairs and the bunks and how hard and PAINFUL it will be for you to get around, they'll make the camp counselors set you up in the infirmary, where you're nowhere near the other kids and you can hang out with your new friend. Oh yeah, and let your foot heal too. Because that's the most important thing.

I wasn't faking—my ankle REALLY hurt, and it was swollen, something I didn't think you *could* fake even if you wanted to. When I'd first come in with Julie, Lisa had frowned as she stared at my face, which was somehow hive-free, but then she'd clued in to how I was leaning on Julie and holding my foot up in the air. She took me into an exam room and felt around my foot and my ankle and even got the camp doctor to come in and look at it to make sure it wasn't broken. Which it wasn't.

I only cried a little, but I let them give me the pain pills because it really did hurt. A lot.

It was almost comforting that they gave me the same room at the infirmary. Just like old times, right? Ha ha! And it was kind of nice to be fussed over. They propped up my wrapped foot, tucking ice packs around it and making sure I was comfortable. Well, as comfortable as I could be, lying there with a sprained ankle.

"You should get some rest, but can I get you anything?" Lisa asked.

"I'm not really tired, and I'm okay, thanks."

She nodded. "How about some company?"

I knew exactly who she meant. I nodded. "Sure."

Only a few minutes later Harry came in.

"Bea!" he said.

"Hi!" I smiled, happy to see him.

"What happened?" He popped up onto the chair, making himself right at home in my room. I liked that.

I told him the story of how I had fallen down in pursuit of the best hiding spot.

"That stinks," he said. "I know just the spot you mean, and that would have been perfect. I'm sorry you didn't win and that you're stuck here now."

I shrugged. "It was just for five bucks at the tuckshop. And anyway, I'm happy to be here."

"You're happy to be in the infirmary?"

I nodded.

He made a face, but it was hard to read what his expression meant.

"What?" he asked, looking at me looking at him.

"What does that face mean?"

"What face?"

I rolled my eyes. "The one you're making. Duh."

"It means I don't understand why you're happy to be here."

"Oh. Sometimes it's hard to know what your expressions mean."

He nodded. "It's the eyebrows. If I had eyebrows, you'd get it."

He was smiling, but still my face heated up. "Sorry," I said.

He blinked. "For what?"

"For bringing up that you don't have eyebrows."

"Uh, Bea, *I* brought it up, and it's not like I don't know. And anyway, eyebrows are like the least of my worries, you know?"

Ugh. How could I be so stupid as to remind him about his cancer?

I looked down at my hands, trying to hold back my embarrassed tears.

"Bea? What's wrong?"

All I could do was shake my head. Then I felt

a movement on the bed, and he was climbing up next to me. "Don't be sad. It's okay!"

He didn't sound upset. I looked at him. He was smiling. "Are you sure?" I asked. "I feel foolish when I talk about…you know." And it felt even weirder for *him* to be comforting *me*. He was the sick one.

"You talking about it doesn't make it more or less true. Not talking about my disease doesn't make it go away. It's okay, Bea, really."

"Honest?"

"Honest." He put his hand on top of mine and gave my fingers a squeeze.

"How long have you had it?"

"All my life."

My heart dropped. "You've had cancer your whole life?"

"Cancer?" He jerked back.

"Don't you have cancer?" I almost choked on the word.

"No. What made you think I have cancer?"

"Your hair...I mean...I thought you were in treatment for..."

"Oh! That makes sense," he said. And somehow he was still smiling, even though this was the most awkward conversation ever. "No, I don't have cancer. I have progeria."

"What does that mean? Is it *like* cancer?"

He shook his head. "It's just this disease. It... makes me look the way I do."

"So you don't go to treatments?"

He shook his head. "I take a lot of pills, but I don't have to go to the hospital too much anymore. Mostly just for checkups."

"So you don't hang out here in the infirmary because you have to?"

"Nope. I told you before, I like it here," he said. "And I like it more since you're here. But I'm sorry you hurt your ankle."

I'm not sorry, I wanted to say.

"Hey, why don't I get my iPad—we can watch *Annie*."

"That would be great!" I said, relieved. And, of course, excited about *Annie*. I could watch it over and over forever.

Twenty minutes later, when I'd just started to wonder if he was going to come back, he walked into the room, a goofy grin on his face. It took me a second to notice that he had two ridiculous arches painted on his forehead.

I barked out a laugh.

"What?" he asked, trying to keep a straight face. But as the "eyebrows" went even farther up his head, I laughed even harder.

"What did you do?" I asked, gasping for breath.

"Isn't this better?" he asked. He wasn't doing a very good job of pretending to be serious.

"You're a goofball," I said. And then he started laughing too.

Lisa stuck her head into the room. "What's going

on in here? It sounds like a couple of hyenas—"
She stopped mid-sentence and snorted, pointing at
Harry. "You! I *knew* you weren't just looking for gum
in my purse! You're going to owe me if you ruined
my good eyeliner."

We tried hard to stop laughing. Lisa told us to
keep it down because *some people* in the infirmary
were actually sick.

After she left, Harry got up on the bed with me
and turned on his iPad.

"Do you know all the *Annie* songs?" he asked.

"Yeah. Every single one. AND all the lines to the
movie too."

"Every line? Not just the songs?"

I nodded. "I've watched it at least a million times."

He looked at me. "And it's not a big deal that
you're not in the play?"

"It's way too late. And it's not like I can dance
now anyway," I said, pointing at my ankle in case he
needed a reminder.

"What about helping out with sets or something?"

"They don't need it," I said, not bothering to tell him the real reason I wasn't involved. "I'm helping design the program though."

"Oh. That's good, I guess. But…"

I looked at him. It was hard to take him seriously with those eyebrows. "What?"

"It just seems weird that you wouldn't want to be in the play."

"I can't."

"Why not?"

"Because I can't, okay? Can we watch the movie?"

"I'm sorry, Bea," he said in a soft voice. "I didn't mean to make you mad."

"It's okay. I just…I can't be around them. Not after what Regan did."

"What did she do?"

"Nothing."

"She must have done *something*."

I exhaled. "Fine, okay? She betrayed me by kissing Jeremy, and they're both in the play."

And then, as I realized what I'd just said, I pulled the top of my shirt up over my face until almost my whole head was inside it, like a turtle retreating into its shell.

"What?"

"Ugh! I like Jeremy, and she knew I liked him, and then I found out she kissed him after rehearsal."

"Oh. That's bad, huh?"

"Yes, that's bad," I said from inside my shirt.

"Why are you hiding?"

"It's embarrassing."

"What's embarrassing?"

I poked my eyes out from my shirt. "Telling you this stuff."

"Why?"

"Because I like a boy."

He blinked. His papery eyelids were so pale, I could see the veins in them. "So? People like other people and then someday they get married and stuff. Why is that embarrassing?"

My face got SO HOT when he mentioned people getting married that I pulled my shirt over my face again.

"Bea?"

"What?"

"Stop that."

"No."

"You're being silly. Tell me about this boy. Summer has just started—you can't have known him that long."

"I know him from home. He's my best friend's brother."

"Oh. So you've had a crush on him for a while. And he kissed Regan."

I nodded, even though my head was still in my shirt.

"So he likes her."

Another nod.

"Bea, come out of there."

I pulled my shirt down.

"Why are you so embarrassed?"

"I don't know."

"Do you still like him even though he likes Regan?"

I shrugged.

"Hmm," he said.

"What does that mean, 'hmm'?"

"It seems silly to like someone who likes someone else."

"You can't choose who you like or make yourself just stop liking them. Haven't you ever liked someone?"

Now it was his turn to blush. "No."

"Oh, right!" I pointed at his red cheeks. "So you're blushing for no reason? You like someone, I can tell."

He looked down at his hands. "It's not like *that*. She's a nurse."

"Lisa?" I whispered.

"No." He shook his head, hands still fidgeting. "She's nice and all, but no. This was a really nice nurse at Sick Kids hospital who was there when I went for my checkups. Her name was Lori. But that's not the same. It wasn't a get-married kind of crush. More like a 'I just want to snuggle up' crush. Does that make sense?"

I thought about it for a second, about him being at the hospital and having a nice person around to hug and make him feel comforted when he needed it. "Yes. That makes sense. But you're right. That's different. Haven't you ever had a crush on a girl in *that way*? Like, someone you wanted to kiss or hold hands with?" My face was getting SUPER hot again, but I forced myself not to hide in my shirt. Especially since his face was still pink too. If we were both embarrassed, it was like we canceled each other out.

"I don't think so."

"You would know it if you had."

"What's it like?"

I barely knew this kid, and he was asking me what having a crush was like? "I thought we were going to watch the movie."

"We are, but please, Bea, I really want to know."

"It's like waking up on your birthday, and you know you're getting something awesome. Or like singing when you know no one can hear you but it just feels good to belt it out, you know?"

He nodded.

"What's your favorite food?" I asked him.

"Uh…" He frowned, obviously not sure where I was going. "Spaghetti and meatballs."

"Really?"

He nodded again. "Yeah. With garlic bread."

"Well, imagine that one moment right before you're going to eat it. That anticipation and that fluttery feeling when it feels like life is perfect. It's like that."

"You're making me hungry," he said.

I looked at him and rolled my eyes, then reached for a tissue. "Wipe those ridiculous eyebrows off."

He wiggled them. "Are you sure?"

I laughed so hard. "Yes, I'm sure."

"Fine." He took the tissue and wiped his brow. "What's kissing like?"

I wanted to hide my face again but managed not to. "I don't know," I said with a shrug. "I've never kissed anyone."

"Oh. Okay. I wonder what it's like. I mean, I've seen it in movies."

"This is a weird conversation, Harry."

"I know."

"So."

"So," he echoed.

"Maybe we should just watch the movie?"

With a nod, Harry picked up his iPad.

Conversation over.

NINETEEN

Three days later, the novelty of being in the infirmary had worn off, and I was bored. Really bored.

I was seriously considering just sucking it up and going back to my cabin. Except for one thing—Harry. We'd watched a lot of movies and played a ton of games and told each other jokes and stories and laughed a lot.

But I was restless, and my ankle was mostly better (even though I *may* have been pretending it wasn't), and I got the feeling my parents were getting very concerned, since they kept calling and asking about my ankle and *that* was getting *really* annoying. And maybe I felt a bit bad about making the injury sound a lot worse than it was, causing them to worry about me more than they needed to.

So I decided I'd give myself one more day to hang out in the infirmary and then go back to the cabin, no matter how much I didn't want to. At least there were fun things to do, and maybe I'd even try waterskiing. Maybe.

I got up to go to the bathroom, not bothering with the crutches because I didn't need them.

Which, as it turned out, was a mistake.

"Bea?" Harry said from the doorway behind me.

I froze with my hand on the bathroom-door handle. "Yeah?"

"You're not limping."

"Oh! Really?" That was my super-intelligent reply.

"And no crutches?"

I had a feeling I was about to be…

"Busted. You're faking!"

"Shhhh," I said, turning around and looking over his shoulder to make sure there wasn't a nurse behind him. "I'm not faking. Not totally."

"What's going on?"

"I have to use the bathroom."

He walked over to the chair beside my bed and hopped up, folding his arms across his chest. "I'll wait."

Awesome.

So I used the bathroom and then came out to see Harry, still sitting there with his arms crossed. I limped a little, not wanting him to think I was a *complete* fraud.

"What movie should we watch?" I asked.

"Why are you faking?" he asked, ignoring my question.

"I'm not. I sprained my ankle."

"Why do you only limp when people are watching?"

I sat on the bed. "Fine. I like it here. I don't get to hang around like you do if I'm not hurt."

"But you're not hurt—you should go be with the kids in your cabin."

I shrugged.

"You're hiding out here, aren't you?" he asked.

Yes. "No!" I looked at him. "I really hurt my ankle."

"Did you? Or did you trip yourself on purpose?"

I couldn't believe he was accusing me of faking the whole entire injury. "I did not. I fell for real and sprained my ankle. I wouldn't have done that on purpose." *Unless maybe I'd thought of it.*

Before he could say more mean things, I got up.

"Where are you going?"

Where *was* I going? I looked around but couldn't come up with anything good. "Away."

"You do that a lot, don't you?"

"What?"

"Run away from stuff when it gets hard."

"I do not!"

He didn't need eyebrows for me to read the *Oh really?* expression on his face.

I sat back down. "I do not," I said again, but it wasn't very convincing.

"You have to face stuff, even if it's scary. If you don't, you're a coward."

Was *he* calling *me* a coward? I couldn't help saying, "You're one to talk! You sit in here all day instead of doing fun camp stuff!"

"That's different! I have a disease that makes me look the way I do. Nobody wants to be around the kid with progeria!"

"*I* want to be around you."

"You're different, Bea. Most people are afraid of me. I don't get to run away from my disease. It's there wherever I turn. Some days...I wish...I just wish I was a normal kid. But I'm not." His big eyes got all glassy, and my heart ached for him.

"People shouldn't be afraid of you. That's not fair," I said. Because it *wasn't* fair. Harry was a cool kid—the coolest kid I knew. He shrugged and wiped at his eyes. "It is what it is, Bea. Life's not fair. If it were, I wouldn't look like this, and I'd be out there with the rest of the kids. But I don't think you should let a couple of mean girls keep you from doing fun stuff. Stop running away, Bea. You don't have a disease. You have nothing to run away from."

"You shouldn't let your disease get in the way of your life either."

He opened his mouth like he was going to say something, but instead closed it and shook his head. More tears came out, and I grabbed a tissue and held it out for him.

"What?" I asked.

"Nothing," he said with another headshake.

"You were going to say something."

"It's nothing," he said, wiping at his tears. "I don't want to talk about it."

I felt bad. "I didn't mean to make you cry, Harry. I'm sorry. I just…I wish…oh, I don't know."

He nodded. "I know. It's okay, Bea. I've made peace with my disease. Believe me. I've even been to a therapist."

Wow. "Really?"

"Sure." He nodded. "Tons of times."

"What's that like?"

He shrugged. "Nothing major. It's nice to have someone outside your family to talk to. You know, about your problems and life and stuff."

"Huh. That doesn't sound so bad."

"It's not. My doctor is a really nice lady. I can tell her lots of stuff I can't tell my parents."

"What kind of stuff?"

He looked at me, and I could tell he was wondering whether he should tell me.

"You can trust me, Harry. I won't tell anyone."

"I know that. It's just…No, I don't want to talk about it anymore."

"Okay." I admit, I was a little hurt that he didn't seem to trust me, but I guess some stuff is private.

Even though I'd told him about Jeremy and my crush, I supposed I couldn't expect him to tell me all his secrets.

"Thanks, Bea. Hey, want to watch *Transformers*?" he asked.

"Not again! And I don't care how much you beg me."

"Fine," he said, hopping down from the chair. "I'll go get my iPad, and you can pick what we watch."

"Even a romantic movie with kissing?"

He pretended to gag. "I might barf, but fine."

He left the room. What he'd said stayed behind, swirling around in my head. *Did* I run from stuff?

I ran from Frankie when she told me she wasn't going to Camp Shalom. I ran from Jeremy when the Tiara Twins embarrassed me, and I was *still* avoiding him. I ran from Regan when she tried to explain what had happened with Jeremy, and now I was hiding out in the infirmary.

And had just tried to run from Harry when he said something I didn't like.

Huh.

Maybe I did run away a lot. Maybe the way I reacted to bad stuff made it worse. Maybe Harry was right, and I needed to find some courage to face the stuff that was hard or made me uncomfortable.

Maybe then I'd be in *Annie* and not just kidding myself that I didn't really want to be.

Because I *really* wanted to be. And helping out with the programs wasn't anywhere near as cool as being in the play.

Of course, now it was too late.

But maybe it wasn't too late to fix the other stuff.

TWENTY

The next day Lisa examined me and gave my ankle the green light. She said I had to take it easy and be sure I didn't put too much weight on my foot before it was completely healed. That meant waterskiing was out, which was a huge relief.

I packed up my stuff and got ready to meet my cabin crew for lunch in the mess hall.

But first I wanted to see Harry.

I heard him come in at his regular time and talk to Lisa about the day's tasks. And then he came into my room.

"What's the buzz, Bea?" he asked, a big smile on his face.

"I'm going back," I blurted out, ignoring his joke.

His face fell. "Home?"

"No, silly." I rolled my eyes. "To my cabin."

"Oh." He hopped up on the bed beside me. "That's good."

I took a deep breath and said, "You were right, Harry. I shouldn't run away from stuff."

He nodded.

"I'll miss hanging out with you though," I said.

"Me too. And *you* were right too, you know."

"About what?"

He looked down at his hands, fidgeting with his fingers. "You said I shouldn't let my disease get in the way of my life."

Oh. That. "I guess we were both right."

He nodded. "I talked with my dad about it. And we talked about ometz lev—about being coura-geous. And how being brave doesn't mean you can't also be scared about doing something. It means doing it anyway. He said that even if something doesn't turn out the way you hope, that's not failing. Not trying at all because you're scared is failing."

That made a lot of sense. "So what are you going to do?"

"I can't do all the activities, but maybe I'll try swimming and arts and crafts and some other stuff. Maybe even zip-lining!" His eyes lit up. "I've always wanted to."

I smiled. "That sounds like fun."

"Yeah. No more hiding."

"And no more running."

We were so serious that we shook hands on it.

"I'll look around for you," I said. "And, of course, I'll come visit during free time."

He gave me a grin. "I'd like that."

"You're a big silver lining, you know," I said.

He tilted his head. "What does that mean?"

"It's an old saying. *Every cloud has a silver lining.* My dad says that when bad stuff happens,

something good is always there too, a silver lining—
you just have to look for it. Like, the silver lining of
being here at the infirmary is getting to hang out
with you."

He nodded. "I get it. It's like that song in *Annie*
when she sings about how the sun will come out
after all the gray and lonely days. Same thing,
right?"

"Exactly like that!" I said, so pleased that Harry
got it.

Lisa suddenly appeared in the doorway. "What
are you two up to?" she asked. "It's awful quiet
in here."

Harry shrugged. "Just talking."

Lisa looked from Harry to me and then smiled.
"Okay, well, it's time to go, Bea. Julie's here."

As I was leaving, Harry grabbed my hand.
I looked at his face—he was blinking hard. "Come
back later, okay? Promise?"

I nodded, blinking hard too, then turned and left.

TWENTY-ONE

Walking into the mess hall was scary. I'd been away from my cabin for what felt like forever, and I didn't really know what to expect. My face felt prickly, but I took a few deep breaths and willed myself NOT to get hives.

Ometz lev...I can do this. I repeated my new mantra over and over to try to make myself believe it.

We were early for lunch, so the rest of the girls hadn't arrived yet. I had my choice of where to sit, so I took the spot next to Julie. It felt safe.

Every second felt like an hour as the squeak of the doors announced new groups of kids filing in. I'd look to see if it was it was the girls from my cabin and let out a breath when it wasn't. I wished my heart would stop racing. Ugh.

Then they *did* arrive. Everyone had wet hair, so they must just have had swimming or waterskiing or maybe kayaking. As they approached the table, I willed myself not to squirm or faint. I thought about Harry, and that gave me the nerve to give Regan a smile. Her eyes went wide in surprise, but I nodded at the spot next to me. I held my breath until I thought my lungs would explode.

She came over but didn't sit down.

I finally exhaled. "Sit with me?" I asked.

That was all the encouragement she needed. She dropped onto the bench. "How are you doing then, Bea?"

"I'm mostly all better."

"I'm glad."

"Regan?" I said, looking into her green eyes.

"Yeah, Bea?"

"We need to talk."

She nodded. "I suppose we do."

And we did. After lunch we walked together to the A&C cabin, and she explained to me what had *really* happened with Jeremy.

As I listened, I grabbed a leaf off a bush we passed and tore it up.

"Like I said, Bea, *he* tried to kiss *me*. I told him I wasn't interested, but that wicked Carly didn't bother to find out the real story. I swear it—I *didn't* kiss him."

"So you promise you don't like him?" I asked, even though it didn't seem as important anymore that she didn't.

"I promise. I didn't like him then, and I don't like him now. I'm just sorry there was such a misunderstanding. AND I'm sorry Carly is such a rotten cabbage!"

"Me too."

"So we're good then?" Regan asked, looking hopefully into my eyes.

I slid my arm across her shoulders. "We're good. And I have so much to tell you."

"Like what?"

I looked around to make sure I wouldn't be overheard, but still leaned as close as I could and whispered right in her ear, "I made a new friend."

She jerked away and looked at my face. "You did? Who?"

"His name is Harry."

"Is he your boyfriend then?"

"It's not like that. We're just really good friends."

Regan nodded. "All right then. Have I seen him around?"

"Probably not. He spends most of his time at the infirmary."

"Is he sick?"

I paused. It was a logical question. "Yes, I mean…no…. I mean, he kind of works there."

"*Works* there?" she asked. "What are you on about then, Bea? You're not telling me you've made friends with a doctor, are you?"

"No," I said, laughing. "He's a kid. He just… he has a disease that makes him look different."

She frowned. "What kind of disease?"

I tried to remember what he'd called it. "Pro something. Progers…no…progeria? I think that's it. It makes him not grow very well. Also he's bald. But I'm really glad I got to know him. He's really funny and smart and likes musicals. We've been hanging out a lot. He spends a lot of time in the infirmary because other kids make fun of him."

"That's awful for him. He sounds lovely."

"Maybe you can come with me to the infirmary at free time to meet him?" I liked the idea of the three of us hanging out.

She shook her head. "I've got rehearsal. The play's less than a week away!"

Oh, right. *Annie* rehearsal. "How's that going?" I asked, because that's what friends do, even when friends are a bit upset that they aren't in the play and even though they ran away from tryouts and it's their own stupid fault.

"It's okay. I'm learning as much as I can—it's a good thing we're not doing every single song from the play, though. I'm wrecked!" She looked around and then whispered, "Jeremy's not really what I'd call star material. And after I told him I don't like him, I think he's sorry he ever tried out."

Of course. Because he'd done it just to be around Regan. Served him right! I just hoped he didn't ruin it for everyone else.

"It would be so much better if you were in it, Bea. It's not as much fun as I thought it would be. It's a lot of hard work, and I keep forgetting some of the lines."

"We can practice if you want. Maybe tonight after Shabbat service."

"That would be grand—thank you."

We got to the A&C cabin and took our spots around the table. Abby came out with a big tub full of leather and all sorts of tools and plopped it on the table.

"Welcome back, Bea. You okay to work on the *Annie* program some more?"

"Yes," I said.

"Great. You can head back to the computer, and I'll be there in a second to put in the password."

I was fine with missing out on today's craft—I'd made leather jewelry at the Jewish Community Center. It's one of those crafts that never turn out as well as you imagine.

Abby gave me the list of everyone who was in the play and showed me a professional playbill she'd found on the internet as a sample design. I told her I'd input in all the names and make the program look good. She left me to get started and returned to the other kids.

Typing in the names and making the program look professional took hardly any time at all. I was going to flag Abby to show her what I'd done, but then I got an idea. I opened a new browser window. There was something I was curious about. I typed *progeria* into the search engine. A bunch of sites came up, but I just clicked on the first one and read a few lines.

Immediately I wished I hadn't.

Oh no.

I wanted to run. Run from the A&C cabin, run from Camp Shalom and, most of all, run from Harry.

But I'd promised. I'd promised him I wouldn't run anymore. And now that I knew the truth about Harry, not running was the hardest thing I'd ever done.

TWENTY-TWO

I went to find Harry during free time, but he wasn't at the infirmary. Lisa said she thought he was at his family's cottage, but that was out-of-bounds for me.

As I walked back to Cabin 17 to maybe write a letter home, I spotted him in the woods, sitting on a stump. He had his iPad on his lap. I was surprised to hear music I recognized.

He was watching *Annie.*

I walked over to him.

He smiled. "Hi!"

"Why didn't you tell me?" I blurted out. The anger bubbling up in me surprised us both.

His eyes went wide. "Tell you what?"

"About progeria."

"I *did* tell you. What's going on, Bea?"

"You didn't tell me you're going to die!"

He looked down at his iPad, the brim of his hat covering his face. "Oh. Did Lisa tell you?"

"I found out on the internet. Does EVERYONE know except me?"

"Bea…" He shook his head and then looked right into my eyes. "Sit down." He moved over a bit so there was room for me on the stump.

"No. I don't want to sit down. I'm mad at you. And I know it's not fair to be mad at you because of—"

"*This*!" he interrupted. "*This* is why!"

Most of the time, Harry was pretty cheerful so the intensity of his words shocked me. He was not kidding around.

"This is why *what*?" I asked.

"*This* is why I didn't tell you. I didn't want to be 'the dying kid' to you. I didn't want you to get all weird and treat me like I was breakable. I wanted you to treat me like a regular kid."

"But you *aren't* a regular kid," I said.

"I was before you found out. You played with a regular kid, you joked around with a regular kid," he said.

I just looked at him. I had never seen him so upset.

Then he whispered, "To *you* I was a regular kid."

I took a breath but couldn't hold back the tears. "I don't understand, Harry," I said through my sobs. "It said the average lifespan is fourteen. FOURTEEN! You're thirteen *NOW*!"

"I KNOW that!" he snapped. "I know it every morning when I wake up. I know that today could be my last day. I've lived with this my whole life. You think I *don't* know?"

My throat was now so tight, I couldn't even speak. *I am such a jerk. How could I be so mean to my new friend? That is not what good friends do.*

I sat down next to him on the stump, put my arm around him and gently pulled him close. "I'm sorry, Harry," I managed to say. "I'm so sorry."

"It's okay. It's not your fault," he said. He was snotty and crying too. "I didn't want you to know. I didn't want you to feel weird around me or sad like you are now. That's why, Bea," he said quietly. "That's why I didn't tell you."

We cried for a long time. Then it occurred to me that we were wasting his very precious time on being sad. And that made me feel worse. If HE could be really brave, I could too.

Taking my arm off his shoulder, I wiped my face on my sleeve. "I'm sorry. That was awful of me. I just…it was a surprise. I couldn't believe you hadn't told me."

He wiped his eyes with his own sleeve. "Do you understand why now though?"

"I do. And I promise I won't be weird to you anymore. At least, I'll try my best, okay?"

Harry nodded. "Okay. No treating me like the dying kid."

"Deal." We even shook on it.

"Watch *Annie* with me?"

"Seriously? You have to ask?"

He started the movie again, and as Annie sang "Tomorrow," I couldn't help but wonder if Harry was thinking about his tomorrow. Or whether he would even get one.

I slid my hand into his and gently squeezed his fingers.

He looked up at me, and I knew what he was thinking. "Oh please," I said, wishing my voice wasn't quite so wobbly. "I'm not holding your hand because you're the dying kid."

But secretly that *was* part of it.

TWENTY-THREE

It was Friday, so before dinner we all put on our white outfits to go to the Shabbat service. It was held at a special outdoor chapel that faced the lake and smelled like pine trees. It was really pretty, and I liked it a lot more than the freezing-cold synagogue at home, where I couldn't see the stage over the old-lady hats.

I was still feeling sad about Harry, though I'd pretended to his face that everything was okay.

But everything was NOT okay. He was going to die. Before he had even grown up. That was SO not okay.

"I'm starving," Regan said as we sat waiting for service to begin.

I nodded, not really in the mood to talk.

"What's wrong?" Regan asked.

"Nothing," I said flatly, not looking at her.

"Don't give me that, Beatrice," she said, my name sounding almost cool with her accent. "You've been quiet since this afternoon. Did you have a fight with Harry or something?"

I swallowed against the sudden lump in my throat and was quiet for another moment, and then I said, "No. It's not like that."

"What is it, Bea? You can tell me." Regan put her hand on my arm, which just made the lump worse. I wanted to tell her, but Harry's secret wasn't mine to tell. I opened my mouth, couldn't think of what I *could* tell her, so shut it and shook my head.

"Are you worried that at the end of the summer, you'll go home and you'll miss him?"

I looked at her and nodded. It was true enough. "I'll miss you too," I said. Missing her would be different though. It would hurt, but it wouldn't be agony the way missing Harry would be if he died. Or, I should say, *when* he died.

"And I'll miss you," Regan said, sliding her arm across my shoulders.

But at least you're not going to die. A sigh escaped me.

I could feel Regan's eyes on me. "Oh, Bea," she said. "Don't be sad now. We have all this time together before the summer's over. We should be happy. It's way too soon to be sad about us not being together."

I looked at my friend and realized she was right. About everything. I shouldn't be sad about losing Harry when he was still here. That would ruin the time we had together. I leaned into her, and she squeezed me into a sideways hug.

"Thanks, Regan," I said.

A few minutes later the two camp directors, Jamie Beth and Ben—Harry's parents—stepped up to the big podium, which was made out of a giant tree stump.

When I'd moaned about coming to a Jewish camp, thinking I'd have to go to lessons and stuff like at Hebrew school, Mom had said that although there were Shabbat services, it was a lot less formal.

She was right. Every Friday, after the two of them greeted us, Jamie Beth would lead us in singing a lot of the prayer songs I already knew. Then Ben would talk about the theme for the week.

Ben was very tall with thick dark hair under his kippah and bushy eyebrows that looked like caterpillars. They were definitely not drawn on. Like Harry, he was really funny and good-natured, and between the singing (which wasn't terrifying because everyone was singing) and his talks, I actually enjoyed the Friday night services.

Last week Ben spoke about kavod, which means honor and respect. He said one of the best ways we can express kavod is by BEHAVING. I think he picked that topic because a bunch of kids had gotten into trouble for taking some sailboats out on the lake when they weren't supposed to. They got caught when they couldn't sail the boats back to shore on their own, and their counselors had to send the powerboat out to save them. We weren't supposed to know, but Regan had heard Penny telling Julie about it when she was brushing her teeth one night.

Regan and I had exchanged knowing glances.

Tonight, after we sang, Jamie Beth wished us a Shabbat Shalom and left the podium.

Ben began, saying that tonight he wanted to talk about ometz lev—courage—and how it can come in many forms. For a second I thought he was talking RIGHT TO ME about how I needed to be brave about Harry and his illness and not run away from him or from anyone else when things got difficult. But then I remembered Harry saying he had talked to his dad a lot about being courageous, and not letting his fears of people being mean keep him from enjoying his life.

As Ben finished his talk, I noticed him beaming a huge smile toward the back of the crowd. I turned and gasped.

There was Harry, standing over to one side, almost hidden in the trees. I knew for a fact that he'd never come to the service before. Jamie Beth was standing behind him with her hands on his shoulders. She looked so happy. I saw her bend down and whisper something in Harry's ear. He nodded and smiled back at her.

Forget Ben's talk. Everything I needed to know about bravery was standing right there in board shorts and a New York Yankees ball cap.

TWENTY-FOUR

It was two days to visitors' day. Which also meant it was two days to *Annie*, something I couldn't forget, thanks to Regan's new hobby, which was FREAKING OUT about *Annie*. Seriously, she was a bigger nervous wreck than even *I* would have been if *I* were the lead. But being a friend meant being supportive and trying not to snap at her, even if I felt like if she said one more time that she was going to pee her pants onstage, I was going to lose it.

It was free time, and we were running through her lines *again*. Her rehearsal had been canceled because of a camp staff meeting. So maybe I was a little mad, because helping her with her lines meant

I couldn't go see Harry. And really, she knew her lines, so going through them eighty-seven million more times wasn't going to help.

"That was perfect," I said after she finished the last scene.

"Really? I didn't miss any words?"

"No." At least, not that I'd noticed. I had drifted a bit in the middle, but I was sure she'd gotten *almost* all, if not all, the words. "You're great. It's going to be great."

"I'm not so sure, Bea." She frowned and held her hands to her stomach. "My guts are feeling very unsure also."

"Your guts are fine—they're just nervous."

"Right. So one more time then?"

I wanted to scream! "Regan, I think if you *over*-practice, you're going to start making mistakes. That happens a lot on Broadway. They say you're only supposed to practice until you know it and then stop."

"Is that right?"

I had no idea—I was totally making it up. And yes, that made me a bad friend, but I just couldn't listen to it anymore. Plus, I had somewhere else I really wanted to be.

"Hey, want to go see Harry?"

"I do. If you're sure I shouldn't practice more…"

"I'm sure."

I knew I'd find Harry at the infirmary—he made sure he was there every day at free time to meet me. He said he was joining activities around the camp, but I hadn't spotted him anywhere. After seeing him at the service, though, I knew he was telling the truth. Plus, we had a deal.

I did look forward to visiting him every day. We'd play on his iPad or just hang out in the woods and tell each other stuff about our lives. Sometimes it felt like I told him more than he told me, but he said he liked hearing about my life and my "normal kid" stories.

I walked through the front door of the infirmary, expecting to see Harry at the desk since he usually did his filing while he waited for me. But instead Lisa and Claudia were sitting there chatting. They looked up as we walked in.

"Hiya, Bea," Lisa said. "Harry's in triage. It's been a slow day."

"I guess that's a good thing, huh?" I said.

"You bet. Gives us girls time to catch up on our academic reading." She held up a glossy celebrity magazine and gave me a wink.

"This is Regan," I said. "Is it okay if we go back?"

"Sure thing. Hi, Regan. You're going to be our Annie, aren't you?"

Regan nodded. "Nice to meet you, and yes, I am. If I don't wet meself from the nerves."

"I think we have some diapers in the back, don't we?" Claudia asked Lisa.

Regan looked horrified.

"We were just kidding, hon. I'm sure you'll do great," Lisa said with a smile and a wink.

"You *will* do great," I added, because friends encourage each other, especially when nurses are teasing them and making them worry EVEN MORE about their upcoming performance. "You've been practicing, and you sound amazing!"

"Thanks, Bea."

I nodded. "Come on—let's go find Harry."

We went through the doorway to the triage area, which was just a fancy name for an exam room.

Harry was lying on one of the beds, stone-still. His hat was off, and for the first time I could see his entire pale, veiny head.

His eyes were open and staring at the ceiling. He wasn't even blinking. He looked like he was… no, he couldn't be…

My heart stopped. "Harry!" I shrieked. "Harry!"

He turned his head and looked at us. "What's going on? Why are you yelling?"

My heart resumed beating. "Were you sleeping?" I asked, trying to sound normal. I knew I couldn't say, *I'm so relieved you're not DEAD. Because for a second there, I was sure you were DEAD.*

He would have hated that.

"No, just thinking." He sat up and put his hat back on. He looked at Regan. "Hi. I'm Harry."

"Regan," she said. "Pleased to meet you."

Harry looked at me and said, "I didn't think you'd be coming today. But I'm glad you did." And then he gave me a big smile.

"I was helping Regan practice for *Annie,*" I said. "But she knows the whole thing perfectly, so I thought I'd bring her to meet you."

"That's great. Let's get outside. It's stuffy in here." Harry hopped off the bed, and as we left the room, I caught Regan staring at him. I wondered what she thought. I'd told her about his disease—except for the dying part, of course. Harry would have hated my telling her that. But she probably hadn't realized just how different he would look.

We went to our special spot in the woods. Regan and I sat on the stump while Harry acted out scenes from *Annie.* He did ALL the parts while we took pictures and videos of him with his iPad. It was hilarious. He hardly knew any of the words and made them up as he went along. Regan and I laughed like lunatics. The best was his Daddy Warbucks. He almost fit the part of the distinguished bald man, but when he tried to make his voice low and commanding, well, it just came out hilarious.

Regan and I had to beg him to stop because we couldn't take any more.

Eventually we had to wipe away our tears of laughter and go meet the rest of our cabin for dinner. But I could tell as we said goodbye to Harry that Regan knew exactly why I liked him so much. He'd won her over too. Before we left, he set his iPad on a timer to take a picture of the three of us. It turned out great. He promised to send us both copies.

Because that's what friends do.

TWENTY-FIVE

Julie met us before we even got to the cabin, a worried look on her face. "What?" I asked. "What's wrong?"

She looked from me to Regan. "It's your grandmother, Regan. She's had a stroke and is in the hospital."

Regan just blinked and stared at Julie.

"Regan?" Julie said, putting her hand on Regan's shoulder.

"Nana! No, can't be. Is she dead?"

"I don't have a lot of details, but no, she's not dead. Your parents are flying over from Ireland, but in the meantime, your uncle Barry is driving up.

He should be here in a couple of hours to get you. We'll have to pack up your stuff—I don't think you'll be coming back."

I put my hand on Regan's back. "I'll help."

"Thanks, Bea," Julie said, leading us to the cabin. "Are you okay, Regan?"

Regan nodded. "I guess so. If she's not dead…I… I don't know."

As we walked, I rubbed her back the way Mom would rub mine if I was sick, in big slow circles. "It's okay," I said, trying to be comforting. "It'll be okay."

Then Regan turned and looked at me. "*Annie.*"

I ignored that because I knew exactly what it meant. I followed Regan into the cabin. Julie led her over to her bunk and sat her down. "We'll pack your stuff," she said.

When we were almost finished, Regan came over to me.

"I finished it," she said, opening her palm to show me the friendship bracelet she'd made for me.

Only then did it really hit me that my friend was leaving. "I didn't finish yours," I squeaked out.

She shook her head and pushed the bracelet into my hand. "It's all right. Give it to Harry when you do."

"You sure?"

She nodded. "Yes." And then she looked right into my eyes. "You'll have to do it, Bea."

"I can't."

Julie looked from her to me and back. "Do what?"

"You have to, Bea. No one else can do it."

"Samantha should do it," I said. "She tried out, and she *wants* to do it."

"Oh. The play," said Julie.

"You wanted to be in it, right?" Regan said. "This is your chance."

I couldn't tell her now that I had planned to blow the audition. "I didn't want such a big role," I said, hoping that would be good enough. "Samantha—"

"Samantha what?" Carly demanded as she and Samantha came over.

I straightened my shoulders, summoning my ometz lev, determined not to be afraid of them any longer. (It helped that Julie was right there beside me.) "Regan's grandmother is sick, and she has to leave. Samantha will have to take over the lead in the play."

Samantha's eyes got as big as saucers. "I can't do that. It's in two days! I don't even know all my Miss Hannigan lines yet."

I rolled my eyes. "You won't need to know Miss Hannigan's lines if you're Annie."

"But there isn't enough time to learn the whole part!"

"You know all the lines, Bea, I know you do," Regan said. "You know all the words to all the songs and, well, if your singing isn't perfect, that's okay."

I'd forgotten that she thought I was a horrible singer. But even though I *wasn't* really a horrible singer, it didn't matter—I couldn't be Annie! "I can't. I can't do it."

"Don't they have understudies?" Julie asked. "In case this kind of thing happens?"

Regan glared at Samantha. "Yes, we do. Samantha was my understudy."

Samantha blushed and looked at the floor. "I didn't think…"

Julie zipped up Regan's suitcase. "We'll worry about that later. Regan, I'll take this to the front gate. You go with the girls to the mess hall for dinner—your uncle won't be here for a while yet, so you may as well eat."

We followed her out of the cabin, and I looped my arm around Regan's. "I'm so sorry about your grandmother," I said. "I hope she's okay."

"Thanks. I hope so too. I don't know her that well since she lives here, so far from home, but I was going to be with them later this summer and I…" Her voice trailed off as she started to cry. I put my arm around her and gave her a big hug.

"I hope she doesn't die, Bea."

I squeezed her close. "Shhhhh. She's going to be okay. You have to hold on to that."

Regan sniffled and nodded. "Thanks, Bea. I hope you're right. Can you promise me one thing?"

I nodded. "Anything."

"Don't let those rotten girls ruin *Annie*."

I sighed. "I don't think I can do it, Regan. I really don't."

"You have to. Samantha will be awful. You know every word, every line, all the songs. You are the best Annie we've got, and you know it. Do it for me, please."

I took a deep breath and then let it out yoga-style, remembering my promise to Harry—no more running. I needed to be brave. "All right. I'll do it. But only for you, NOT for those horrible Tiara Twins."

"Good. You'll be a great Annie. And I'm not just saying that because you're my best friend."

My heart gave a little jump. "Your best friend besides Taffy?"

"No, Bea. My best friend. Period."

I thought about Frankie for a moment. Maybe there were different kinds of besties for all the different parts of your life. I threw my arms around Regan again. "You're my best friend too. I hate that you live so far away."

"We'll write letters and video chat," she said into my ear.

"Of course we will." It wouldn't be the same, but… "And someday, maybe, I'll even get to visit you in Ireland."

"That would be grand, Bea. Just grand."

TWENTY-SIX

I stood in the wings where the audience couldn't see me. I was SO nervous, I started to wonder if the nurses really did have diapers at the infirmary and if they'd show under my costume if I got some. You know, just in case.

I peeked out from behind the curtain. That might have been a mistake. The lodge was full, and I mean FULL. And not only was the whole camp out there, but also my parents and even Stevie. I could tell by the energy in the room that everyone was eager for the show to start.

"Do you see my parents?" Jeremy asked from behind me.

"Yeah, they're sitting with mine," I whispered, squinting for a better look. "Ugh, and your dad has his camera out. The fancy one with the big lens."

"I've never been so nervous, Bea," he said. "How are you so calm?"

"Calm?" I said in a slightly screechy voice. "You think I'm calm? Look at me!" I stared at him while his eyes scanned my face.

"The hives don't look that bad," he said.

I snorted. "Only because Penny put, like, ten pounds of makeup on me. Believe me, they're bad." My face had been prickly since I'd started rehearsing, and I couldn't take the medicine because it would make me drowsy. I had to be sharp if I was going to pull this off. If that meant I was going to be a spotty Annie, so be it. Maybe from where the audience sat, the hives would look like freckles. I couldn't worry about that now. I was going to need all my courage just to step onstage.

THE SUN WILL COME OUT

"How are you doing, kids?" a deep voice said from behind us. I turned to see Ben, holding a microphone in his hand. He was the MC and would be welcoming all the families for visitors' day and then introducing the show.

"Good," Jeremy said, though his voice sounded a little strangled. I knew just how he felt.

"Ready to get started?"

No. "Uh, yeah. Of course." *Breathe, Bea. Let's ometz lev the heck out of this.*

Ben squatted down in front of me so he was at eye level with me. "Bea. Jamie Beth and I want to thank you for what you've done for Harry and for all the chesed—the kindness—you've shown him."

I wasn't exactly sure what he meant, but I said, "You're welcome. He's a great guy. I like him a lot."

Ben smiled and put his hand on my shoulder. "He likes you a lot too. And he told me he wouldn't miss seeing you as Annie for the world. He has never come to a camp play before, no matter how much we've tried to encourage him. That says a lot about how he feels about you."

"He's here?" I peeked out at the audience again. There he was in the front row, sitting between Lisa and Claudia, a huge grin on his face.

I gave him a little wave. He gave me a double thumbs-up.

"Well, now I'm even more nervous."

Ben laughed and squeezed my shoulder before he stood up. "He's a very lucky boy to have you as a friend," he said.

Which is weird, because I felt like the lucky one.

EPILOGUE

Since I'm still here telling you this story, I guess you've figured out that I didn't die of stage fright. I'm also happy to say that I didn't pee my pants, trip or even faint onstage. I did flub a few lines, but no one seemed to notice. I mean, when I watch the video at home, *I* can tell, but no one in the audience laughed or anything. When they weren't supposed to, I mean.

I sang my heart out. And you know what? I sounded pretty good. Not as good as in the movie version, but for a kid with very little practice and hives all over her face? Not bad at all. I even got a standing ovation, and not just from my parents, either; everyone stood and clapped for me like I was a real Broadway star.

I'm pretty sure Harry down in the front row clapped the hardest.

I might try out for school theater—nothing as big as a lead, because that would be a little more stress than I want. But being Annie did give me the confidence to try out for smaller roles, so that's a silver lining.

Frankie came home from Circle M and was actually jealous that I got to be the lead in *Annie*! She wasn't so sure she wanted to live on a farm anymore, and she said her summer would have been better if we'd been together, which felt kind of like an apology, so I forgave her for ditching me. We're pretty much back to normal now. I didn't fill her in on the whole drama with her brother, especially the part about the non-kiss. I also didn't tell her that I have someone on the other side of the world who I also think of as my best friend.

A person can have two best friends. Or maybe even three.

Oh, and you'll be glad to know that Regan's grandmother made a full recovery, and the whole family got to spend the rest of the summer together before Regan and her parents went home to Ireland. Regan and I video chat all the time now.

We did have that one awkward conversation after she saw the video of my performance. I had to explain how I really can sing and confessed why I had pretended I couldn't. She shook her head, her curls springing around as she laughed, and called me a cabbage. But then she said that I was her favorite cabbage so it was all good.

She even sent me a letter with a hoofprint from Taffy. It's hanging on my wall next to the selfie Harry took of the three of us. Regan's going to send me an invitation to her bat mitzvah, which will be next summer right before camp starts. And the best news? It's going to be here, so I'll be able to attend, and then we'll spend the summer together at Camp Shalom!

My bat mitzvah will be in the fall, so she probably won't be able to come, but we're working on it—her grandparents are already on board, so maybe…

And then there's Harry. We video chat all the time too. He's at camp most of the time because his family lives there year-round. But he also goes to the hospital and stays there sometimes because he's now in a new drug trial. He says the medicine is making him feel a lot better and gain weight. He even had to re-tie the friendship bracelet I'd made him because it got too tight for his wrist.

If he knows I'm having a bad day or thinks I'm feeling sad, he'll draw on eyebrows (or that one time—a moustache!) when we chat online, just to make me laugh. Or he'll sing "Tomorrow" and make up the words as he goes along.

Like, last night it was, "Burrito, burrito, I love ya, burrito, you're always a fart away."

Okay, so he's not always the most *mature* guy ever. But he makes me laugh like no one else can. He's the best kind of friend anyone could ask for. Today, tomorrow, every day, he's my silver lining.

And I'm pretty sure I'm his too.

AUTHOR'S NOTE

Harry is a fictional character, but progeria is a very real disease. For more information and to meet some of the amazing kids affected by this rare genetic condition, please check out the Progeria Research Foundation.

ACKNOWLEDGMENTS

Fun fact: The book you just read has a very long history. I typed the first word sometime back in 2012. It got put on the shelf (unfinished) in 2013 after I lost my mom and didn't feel inspired to write for a time. Eventually I got back to it and completed the manuscript, something I think my mom would have been happy about.

Along the way, several people read it, offering advice, insight and encouragement that was absolutely invaluable. For those early reads and help, a huge thanks to Kate Messner, Jennifer Nielsen, Eileen Cook and Caryn Wiseman. (If you read this book as a rough manuscript and weren't mentioned above, my sincerest apologies and heartfelt thanks—I had a computer meltdown in 2019 and lost all my manuscript notes. *GAH!* Acknowledgments are *SO HARD*, and technology is *THE WORST*.

Once I finished the book, then called *Queen Bea Makes a Buzz*, it got shopped to publishers. It didn't sell. It got shopped again and didn't sell. I put it away, thinking it wouldn't sell ever. If you're not a writer, you may be surprised to hear that a lot of books get written but don't get published. Many (Most? All?) authors have an unsold book (or eight) hidden away somewhere.

Sidebar: *NEVER* give up!

But then there came a day when I heard that PJ Our Way was looking for middle-grade books to include in their amazing program, in which they distribute books to Jewish kids for free. They had already sent out my first book, *Small Medium at Large*, to their subscribing kids, so I knew about their awesomeness. Thinking my book would be a good fit, I dusted off the manuscript, gave it a good edit and sent it in. Fast-forward several months, and they decided to include the book in their catalog.

Without the wonderful and supportive people at PJ Library and PJ Our Way, this book would never have seen the light of day. Thanks to Catriella Freedman, Meredith Lewis, Rachel Goodman and, of course, Harold Grinspoon and Diane Troderman. Thank you, thank you, thank you— for what you've done to support me as an author but even more for supporting young readers, for helping Jewish kids see themselves in books and for sparking joy in reading. You have shaped many lives in ways you can't even imagine, and I am forever grateful.

Even after the book sold to Orca Book Publishers, the work didn't end. Big thanks to Andrew Wooldridge for your support of me and other Canadian authors, putting diverse, representative, important and entertaining books in the hands of young readers.

To the rest of the team at Orca that makes me

so proud to be swimming with your pod: Ruth, Olivia, Kennedy, Susan, Leslie, Vivian and everyone else who had a hand in making this book.

A giant, squealy thank-you to illustrator Brayden Sato and designer Rachel Page for their amazing interpretation of the book that became one of the sweetest, most perfect covers ever. Is it weird that I burst into tears when I saw that selfie that would go on the back? Well, whatever—it means you did a perfect job.

Wait. Did you think I could ever forget you, Tanya, best editor ever? You deserve your very own paragraph. As always, you were a joy to work with on this book. Your insight was right on and nowhere as mean as you promised. Here's to many more in the future. Someday we will celebrate together, for real, with cake and chips and all things carby.

Thank you to Noa Daniel and Shira Kates for helping me with some of the Jewish, Hebrew and summer-camp details.

To my new friend at the Progeria Research Foundation, Eleanor Maillie, thank you for reading a draft of this book for accuracy and for making sure I portrayed Harry authentically and respectfully. Any persisting errors on that front are my own.

Thank you to Hilary McMahon, agent extraordinaire and all-around lovely human being for taking Bea (and me!) on. Here's to many, many more contracts together.

And, as always, I have to thank my home team, starting with husband, Deke, for his never-wavering support of me and everything I do. For being the best chauffeur, bag-holder, tech support and behind-the-scenes guy any author and human could ever ask for, thank you.

Last and probably least, the ragtag group of nonhuman co-workers who are both a help and a hindrance to my writing. I'm looking at you, cats who sit on my laptop when I get up to get a coffee refill, bird who beeps incessantly until I want to scream and dog who needs to be let out (and in, and out, and in) constantly. I would have been done with these acknowledgments twenty minutes ago if not for all of you. Good thing you're all cute.

JOANNE LEVY is the author of a number of books for young people, including *Double Trouble* and *Fish Out of Water* in the Orca Currents line, the middle-grade novels *Crushing It* and the Red Maple Award–nominated *Small Medium At Large*. She lives in Clinton, Ontario.